Kings and Monsters

Three Fates Mafia
Book Four

Clio Evans

Copyright © 2024 Clio Evans

Cover Illustration by Jemlin (@jemlin_c)

Character art illustrated by @jemlin_c

Edited by @sarahinwanderland

All rights reserved. No part of this book may be reproduced or used in any manner without the prior written permission of the copyright owner, except for the use of brief quotations in a book review.

"Cock" was used 180 times in this book.

Do with that what you will.

Cock, cock, cock. (183)

Mortals Beware

Mortals Beware:
In this story, you will find the following:

Primal hunting, size difference, choking, pierced cocks, ball gags, switch dynamics, muzzles, blindfolds, handcuffs, collaring, leashing, impact play, breeding kinks, begging, flogging, nipple play, nipple pumps, frotting, copious amount of cum, decapitation, murder, violence, and more.

If you have any questions, you can reach me on Instagram or Facebook, or via email clioevansauthor@gmail.com

Prologue

Ryan

"That's a good boy," I grunted.

My head fell back as the masked man fit his mouth around my cock. He worshiped my piercings with his talented tongue, sucking on the ring around the tip. My muscles and bones were bathed in fire, struggling against the human form magic temporarily lent me, but I'd hold on as long as possible if it meant getting head like this.

"You feel so fucking good," I groaned.

One day, the Fates would let me be like the other monsters in this godsforsaken city. Then, I wouldn't have to make shady deals for pathetic crumbs.

My gaze shifted to the amulet around my neck, a trinket from a hateful goddess I'd done some nasty work for. Getting enough magic to come to the club had already cost me so much. I was being hunted, but for tonight, I was safe. The amulet burned bright purple, glimmering in the dark corner we sat in.

No one would bother the two of us. They were too busy dancing and getting wasted.

Fuck. I thrust my hips up as the bass of the club music thumped in my veins. The man groaned around me, taking me deeper. I cursed under my breath and gripped his head, holding him still as I fucked his throat harder.

Pleasure coursed through me. I wanted to stay like this all night, giving into my desires.

Nails raked down my thighs, the sharp pain reminding me I had to be careful. He was a human, and I didn't want to accidentally harm him.

I released him, allowing him to breathe.

"I want more," he rasped.

So needy.

The thing was, I was too.

The eyes behind the bronze horned mask smoldered with dark lust. Normally, I would say no. I was already pushing it by using up the magic of the amulet.

But I wanted him.

Desperately.

I wanted to be touched. I *needed* to be wanted.

"Where?" I asked. "I don't want to fuck out here in the open." I couldn't risk exposing myself as a monster.

"There's a room in the back," he said quickly.

I didn't ask how he knew that. I asked nothing, because I didn't care. All I wanted was to be buried deep inside of him, pounding out my frustrations.

The Labyrinth was known for its sex and kink parties, which was why I was here in the first place. Occasionally, I heard a scream of pain from someone being flogged or spanked or gods knew what else. The energy was addicting, the scent of desire like a heavy drug.

He pushed my cock back in my pants, pulled me to standing, and led me through the gyrating crowd.

A heavy beat pulsed through the sex club, vibrating the walls and floor. Lights flashed in a series of brilliant colors, highlighting the humans around us as he pulled me down a hall. He wore black pants and a harness around his broad chest and soft belly. His calloused hand felt good in mine.

I could smell the sex. Even pretending to be a human, my senses were still alive. Beneath the music, there were the cries and groans of ecstasy, some out in the open and others hidden behind closed doors.

My cock strained against my pants, wanting more attention.

Wanting *his* attention.

"Here," he said, gesturing to a red door. "No one ever uses this room."

"Why?" I asked warily.

He shrugged and smirked. "They say there are ghosts in here, but they don't bother me."

I didn't care either. It's not like a ghost was going to fuck with a Minotaur.

He spun and dragged me into a kiss. Our tongues fought as I shoved him through the doorway, pushing the door closed behind us. The air was cooler in here, the music muffled. His hand slipped down to my pants again, undoing them quickly.

"Fuck," I rasped the moment he gripped me.

"You're so big," he moaned.

He had no idea. Even now, my cock felt suppressed in this form, aching for a true release.

I pushed him back onto the plush bed that waited for us.

"Take off your mask and pants," I told him.

He smirked as I gripped my cock and stroked. He undressed for me, kicking his boots and pants off. He reached up, pulling the horned mask off.

Everything about him turned me on. I couldn't remember the last time I'd felt this strongly about a human, but then again...it had been so long since I'd been touched.

He leaned across the bed and grabbed a bottle of lube and condoms in a basket on the side table. My cock throbbed against my palm as I went to the edge of the bed.

"Do you want to fuck me?" he asked.

"More than you know," I growled.

He chuckled as he pushed my hand away, taking control of my cock again. My head fell back as he tore the condom open and fit it over me, dripping lube over my shaft and stroking up and down. He cupped my balls, making a low whistle.

"They're so full," he whispered. "How long has it been for you, hmm?"

"Too fucking long. Lay down and pull your legs back, human."

"*Human*," he snorted, but he was already getting into position.

His cock was stiff as he pulled his legs back. I took the bottle of lube and dripped it over his hole, working him with two of my fingers. He grunted, his eyes fluttering.

"You're too tight," I said. "I'm going to destroy you."

"I'll live," he chuckled. "If I have to crawl to work tomorrow, I will."

"Remember you said that," I teased.

I pressed the head of my cock against him and thrust forward. He cried out, squeezing me so fucking tight that I paused, fighting the urge to come right then and there. I was already so close to the edge that it was almost painful.

"*Whoa*," he rasped, his eyes widening at me.

"What?" I asked, pushing more inside of him.

"I must be seeing things," he grunted. "You looked like a monster for a moment. Don't stop. I want this."

I scowled. I should have stopped, but I was already halfway inside of him, and the pleasure was too great. I leaned over him, planting my hands to either side of his head as I rammed my hips, forcing more into him.

He moaned, and I stifled it with another hungry kiss. He wrapped his arms around me as I started thrusting in and out, his body taking me easier. Over and over, I lost myself in him, my blood burning with fire.

"Harder," he rasped.

"Harder and I'll fucking break you," I whispered.

"I can take you."

He shouldn't have been able to. I fucked him powerfully enough that I felt the alarm bells through my mind, but I didn't stop. He moaned as he held onto me. Our skin slapping together echoed through the room, the muted bass pumping around us in sync. The bed creaked beneath us, the frame threatening to snap, but I didn't care.

My bones burned hotter, and I gasped as I felt a sudden release, but not from my cock.

I looked down, realizing that the amulet had snapped free.

No, no, no.

"Stay still," I growled.

There was no going back now.

He froze beneath me, his eyes widening as I changed. There was nothing I could do. A wave of guilt and concern flooded me as he cried out, my cock growing inside of him, filling him more than he'd ever been before.

"Fuck!" he roared, but he didn't fight me.

Hot cum splashed against my monstrous body as the bed gave way. Suddenly, I was a massive Minotaur again, with a human pinned beneath me on a broken bed. He was over six feet tall and thick, but he felt small compared to me. I almost filled the entire room, the tips of my horns brushing against the ceiling if I straightened.

"Don't stop," he huffed.

"*What?*" I growled. I stared down at him, wondering if I'd heard him wrong. "I'm a fucking monster."

"I said don't fucking stop."

"You're crazy," I whispered. "I'm a Minotaur."

His eyes flew open. "Don't. Stop."

Fuck it. I thrust fully into him.

He moaned, writhing as he took more of me. I felt a sense of awe, and the awe turned into a lust so primal that every concern burned away.

Smoke curled from my nostrils as I wrapped my bulky arms around him and lifted, using him like my own fuck toy. He reached up, his fingers digging into my chest as I bounced him up and down, filling him over and over.

I shoved him against a wall so hard it rumbled.

"You crazy bastard," I huffed.

I breathed in his scent, my eyes closing as I took him. The need to breed him, to fill him with everything I had—I couldn't escape it. It was like he'd worked his way into my soul and had taken control of me, demanding that I breed him.

My movements became deeper and slower. I savored every thrust. Every moan and cry.

He came again, his hot cum shooting over me. That was enough to send me over the edge, too. I groaned as I gave one last pump, a roar leaving me as I came.

Hot seed gushed inside of him, branding him as mine. Even

if we were never together again. I looked down, grunting as I kept filling him. His eyes flashed like silver coins, his cheeks flushed.

For a moment, I forgot I was a hunted and hated monster. I let myself be with him, even if after tonight—we'd never see each other again.

Chapter 1

Talking Heads

Six Months Later

Grim

Stumbling across a dead body was, at the very most, supposed to be a once in a lifetime event.

Yet here I was. A regular Monday, at my regular job, with my regular boss decapitated in his office. His head sat on his desk, blood pooled over everything. BEWARE was painted in stark red on the wall. What amazed me most was that his expression managed to stay frozen in a grouchy scowl.

Even dead, the guy looked like an asshole.

What a way to go.

With a name like Grim, maybe I was just living up to it.

Maybe I was cursed. I wasn't sure anymore. I'd stopped worrying about it years ago. I was almost 32, and in those three decades of life, found at least a body a year. The last six months, bad things had ramped up. I was practically stumbling over dead people.

Death put the *D* in determined.

I should have felt a hell of a lot worse about the body sitting in front of me. Then again, it wasn't like I was the one that killed him.

There was a generic motivational poster on the wall behind the slumped corpse with a bald eagle flying over some trees, a quote about attitude and altitude and how those impacted your life—all covered in his blood.

That poster really hadn't done him much good.

I couldn't help but laugh. It was ironic.

"Fuck me," I sighed, sobering up.

This was a mess.

I shoved my hand into my jeans pocket and pulled out my phone. I made the call to the police station and leaned against the door frame.

"Is this that Grim guy?" they asked.

"Uh...no," I lied, glaring out at the shop.

I coughed and adjusted my voice, leaning into a fake accent. I pretended I was from Louisiana as I answered their questions. *Brandon's Auto Shop. Over on the piers. No idea who else was here. Nope, I don't know him.* We fixed up expensive cars and motorcycles here for clients I never bothered to ask Brandon about. I'd never cared who we worked for.

Now, I wondered if maybe I should have.

They wanted me to stay on the phone with them, but that wasn't happening. I needed to put on my acting chops first. I ended the call and shook my head.

I needed to fake some tears. Or shock. Something. Especially with my track record.

At this point, the Moirai City cops were becoming familiar with my name and I'd only been here six months. One city to the next, but death always found me. It was probably time to move on.

"*Hello?* Is this thing working?"

"Hello?" I called out, looking around the corner.

The shop was silent. I stared at the halfway put together cars and bikes, the towers of scrap metal and random shit that created a maze of metal and tires. It smelled like grease, cleaners, and blood.

I didn't see or hear anyone.

I was already over today. Frustration rolled through me and I shook my head, wondering what the hell I was going to do.

"Ope! There he is. The big problem. Your father sends his regards. Congrats, you're a demigod."

The voice being so close startled me enough that I jumped. I spun around, my heart pounding as I looked for whomever the voice belonged to.

"Hello?" I called out. There was no way they'd gotten here so fast unless someone was close by. "Officer?"

"HAHAH, *officer*. Nope. Over here, asshole."

What the fuck?

I spun again and stared into Brandon's office. The lights flickered ominously, shining a flashing yellow spotlight on the desk.

The head's eyes were *open*.

Horror and curiosity hit me at the same time as his mouth pulled into a disgusting grin. Some of his teeth were broken, and more blood dribbled out.

"Holy fuck," I hissed, taking a step back despite my grotesque interest. It wasn't every day I saw a talking head, which either meant I'd truly lost it, or something bizarre was happening. I opted for the first, considering my history over the last few months. "This has gone too far. I'm seeing shit now."

"Yeah, yeah. Hi, hello, I know this is hard for your brain to comprehend. But it's really a miracle you've made it this long, man."

The talking head cackled like a witch and then spat, shooting a loogie of blood and saliva on the floor. *Gross*. His howling laugh almost sounded like Brandon's, but not quite. In fact, I was sure I'd never heard that guy laugh anyway.

Bottom line, I didn't get paid enough for this. And I'd clearly been drugged. Maybe they were putting acid in the cinnamon rolls at Moonie's now. Self-consciously, I reached up and ruffled my beard for any stray pieces of icing.

"You must have a lot of questions. Luckily, I'm here to answer them."

I stared at the head for a moment, contemplating my choices. The cops were going to be here any minute. Self preservation kicked in. "Fuck this," I said, raising my hands. "I'm out."

"Wait, wait, wait! Didn't you hear me?! Your father is a god! And he has a message for you!"

I stared at him, and he stared at me.

"YOU'RE IN DANGER!" he shouted.

I shook my head. I wanted nothing to do with this. "You've got the wrong guy," I said, taking a step back. "I don't want anything to do with all of this."

"You're Grim, right? Don't you want to know why you keep finding bodies? Don't you want to know why your boss is dead or why you've lived a life of misery?"

I glowered at him. Fuck this.

"Nope," I said. "Not in the slightest."

"Hey!"

I ignored the voice and practically sprinted to one of the garage doors that was open. Sirens howled into the cool dawn, the sun breaking the horizon over the shimmering water. The old garage was set on the piers, buried in the middle of scrap yards and warehouses and gods knew what else.

Leaving the scene was the worst thing I could do, but if the police caught up to me, I'd blame it on shock. *Another body I found!* Yeah, that angle would have to work.

Mentally, I walked through my plan as I grabbed my bike helmet and slipped it on. I zipped up my leather jacket, my figure reflecting from my motorcycle. I was a big guy. Six foot five inches, soft stomach, firm muscles, black beard, and slicked back hair. I was intimidating to most.

Damn it, they're going to think I killed Brandon. Seven bodies in six months...

I sighed and mounted my bike, kicking on the motor. The sirens grew closer as I peeled out, the tires sputtering gravel and dirt as I took off. I weaved through the old buildings that made up this district, taking a route the cops were least likely to use. They'd want a direct path to the shop.

I leaned into my motorcycle and cursed to myself. Exhaustion was starting to catch up to me. At some point, I'd get into a lot of trouble. The sort that quick thinking or smooth talking wouldn't get me out of.

A svelte black crow swooped out of nowhere and landed on one of my handlebars. "Go," I hissed as I batted at it, but it cocked its head, parting its beak to speak.

"You're making my job really fucking tough today, kid," the bird said. "Gotta say I really don't appreciate it."

I gawked at the crow and swatted at it again.

"Go away," I snarled. "Leave me alone! I don't want this!"

Surely, I was still hallucinating. A talking head, a talking bird, the mention of demigods. Did I drink too much last night? Maybe that's what was happening.

I slowed to a regular speed as several squad cars raced past me. I kept my eyes off them and the moment they were far enough away, I rotated the throttle hard. I sped down an empty street, ran a red light, and merged onto the highway.

Cold sweat iced the back of my neck.

"You're in danger!" the bird screeched. *"Danger! Danger! Danger!"*

I smacked it sharply enough that it finally flew up into the air, screeching profanities at me as I raced down the road. What in the Edgar Allan Poe was that shit?

A howl broke through the air, rising above the wind and the rumble of cars around me. My heart hammered faster, the feeling of dread clawing at my back.

The crow still followed me, swooping around my head. I forced myself to breathe as I gripped the handles, weaving between cars as traffic began to slow.

My instincts were in overdrive. I was running from something—maybe I was shocked from finding that body.

Maybe I was in shock from seeing his decapitated head talk.

Maybe it was the fucking talking crow.

Fuck my life.

Another howl echoed from behind me as the traffic slowed. People honked at me as I zoomed between them. I made my way to the side of the road, not caring how many honks or curses I got.

Something was after me. Every part of my body felt alive with the same feeling—drive. As fast and as far as I could.

I wasn't sure what I'd done to make this happen, but this had to be the worst Monday in history.

I glanced at my mirror and regretted it.

Running behind me seemed to be a pack of wolves. Only—their eyes were burning red and they were the size of fucking cars. Their bodies were unnatural. Gears and cogs twisted into their seamless forms, creating the appearance of monsters. Even if their bodies appeared to be man made, they were clearly alive.

And no one else seemed bothered by them?

One of them leapt onto the top of a semi truck, the metal creaking. I caught a glimpse of the driver. Bastard was completely oblivious to the monster on top of his ride.

They hunted as a pack, a chilling howl getting closer, followed by growls that made me want to piss myself.

"Danger! Danger! Danger!" The crow screeched over and over like a warning signing. "You're gonna die, kid!"

"I know!" I barked out, leaning down and going faster. "Fucking shut up!"

The hair on the back of my neck stood up. I was pushing ninety now, and it was doing nothing. I focused ahead of me, making a last-minute decision to take a different route. If I could lose them on the overpass, I could make it to the train station and maybe get away. I'd take the first ticket out of this personal hell.

I took an exit onto a ramp, one that went over several others, stretching up towards the sky. The clouds were turning light pink as the sun continued to rise.

I made the mistake of glancing in my mirror again. The damn mechanical creatures were right behind me.

"Damn it!"

A lot of things happened at once.

One creature leapt, and I jerked my bike, but the two of us were coming to the curve of the ramp before it descended, and making that move was the wrong thing to do. I screamed as the monster crashed into me, hurling me off the bike.

And then I was flying.

Except I didn't have wings.

And the flying was actually falling.

I screamed as I caught a glimpse of the crow above me, a stark black against the pastel sky.

Probably the last sunrise I'd ever see and it was pretty mediocre.

The pain came, followed by nothing but darkness.

Chapter 2

It's Raining Men

Ryan

When I looked in the mirror and saw a human's face looking back at me, every struggle that I faced in the last few centuries felt worth it.

Moving through this world as a monster everyone hated and feared was difficult, and the human cloak I wore was my ticket to freedom.

It wasn't that I preferred to look human. I knew I wasn't a mortal. I never would be. I was the great Minoan Bull, hunted by countless demigods and originally the abominable beast of the Labyrinth. *That* was who I was, but that didn't fit in a world of mafia, wealth, cities, and technology.

I adjusted my black suit and took one last glance over. I was tall and muscled, with short blond hair and a smooth face. It differed from the mortal form I'd worn briefly when doing dirty work for an evil goddess. Even better, it was permanent. The infamous Three Fates Mafia sigil branded my throat, a claim laid on me by the Fates themselves.

To this world, I was Ryan Maddock. An up-and-coming millionaire with multiple companies who owned parts of this city, even if the mortals didn't realize it. At least a hundred men worked for me, and that number was growing the longer I stayed in my role as a mafia boss.

Over nine million people lived in this city. It was split up into ten parts which were ruled by demigods and monsters, some of which overlapped more than others. I turned and looked out the high-rise window, staring down below. Moirai was coming to life as the sun rose. A writhing, oblivious mess.

I felt like a god standing here.

The meeting this morning would be the first where they treated me fully as a member of the Three Fates Mafia. As in, acknowledged by all the *other* branches.

They wouldn't be able to ignore me now.

There was Cerberus, which comprised of three men who could turn into the infamous Underworld monster. Their mate was a demigod named Ashley, daughter of Hermes. Damon, the leader of Cerberus, had been instrumental in the last couple of months of showing me the ropes. Much of what I'd learned was thanks to him, Minos, or Aaecus.

There was the Colchian Dragon, also known as Ian, and his demigod mate Serena. Together, they were with a human mate named Luca. Recently, they had twins, a boy and a girl that looked human but were assuredly not based on them supposedly crying once and breathing fire out of their throats—singeing their human father's hair. Ian, even being a tired new father, showed me a lot of kindness despite the things I'd done in the past.

There were the Chimera twins. They were bastards.

There were the Hydras who, like Cerberus, were made of three men—each one of them more twisted than the other. I avoided them when I could.

The final two demigod branches belonged to Orpheus and Theseus. I hated them the most, especially Theseus. Our history was long and bloody and horrific.

Damon and Ian had done their best over the last couple months to show me everything they could with the business side of things. It had taken some time to fully adjust to my role, but they taught me well. Ian was more patient than Damon, but Damon knew how to make things happen immediately.

While they both were mated to demigods, they were likable. Ashley and Serena were not like the elder demigods, who were absolute bastards.

Then there was Percy. She and Madeline had truly disappeared, and I'd done my best to keep some of their businesses the same out of respect for their time in the Three Fates Mafia —especially the bars downtown. I'd taken over their share, although parts of it were to be divided between all of us, unless the Fates gave us another demigod.

I thought about Percy and Madeline, keeping the guilt at bay. I'd been responsible for causing them a lot of pain, a tool used by a jealous goddess. But in the end, they'd forgiven me. Percy let me live, and the Fates finally gave me what I'd begged so long for.

A place in this world.

A world of monsters, demigods, wealth, power, and bloodshed.

I flexed my hand, thinking about the meeting today. It would be difficult. Not everyone was accepting of the position I'd been given. It didn't matter that I'd spent centuries proving that I was capable.

"Sir, your car is ready."

I looked up, startled by the presence of another. His name was Jeff, and he was one of three men whose name I remembered. Some of their faces were more familiar, but overall, they blended together.

That was currently my biggest fault, but I hoped with time, it would become easier to build connections. I was just rusty at it.

And regardless, they were loyal. In the beginning, there were a couple of brief issues I'd ended with...well, death, but otherwise, things had been smooth.

The last few months had been far less bloody than any time I could think of in my long life.

"Sir?"

"I'm ready," I grunted.

It was a change for someone not to run away from me. Although humans in this day and age seemed less likely to. A one-night stand months ago proved that much.

I followed him out of my apartment. My setup was like Damon's, which I'd done on purpose since I envied the Cerberus penthouse. This flat was at the very top of this building, which was on the east side of the city instead of the middle. Still, I enjoyed good views, and I liked this part of the city better.

We took the elevator all the way down to the parking garage. He escorted me to a sleek black car that waited and opened the door for me. Another guard sat near the opposite window.

"Good morning, sir," the driver greeted me.

I nodded. That was my answer to people that spoke to me unless I had to actually say something.

"We should arrive on time for the meeting," he said.

"I picked up your coffee and breakfast from Moonie's," the

guard said, handing me a small bag and to-go cup. "Jeff made sure of it."

"Thanks." That made me smile. I grabbed the cup and balanced the bag on my lap, peeking inside. Moonie's was a small cafe with the best damn cinnamon buns in the entire world.

I leaned back into the soft leather seat as I feasted on the roll and coffee. This was what it felt like to be a modern man, right? I stared out the window as the car lurched, pulling out of the parking garage and into traffic.

The meeting today shouldn't have been a big deal, but it felt like it. There would be enemies in the same room as me. Theseus and I went so far back that memories became a blur. I still hated him and he had every right to still hate me.

And then the Chimera Twins...

I'd done a lot of dirty work for them. When you're a monster but not chosen by the Three Fates Mafia, you become a tool for them and that's it. There were other monsters in the world, but they didn't have the power that I now had.

Money, respect, power.

The twins no longer had any control over me, but I wasn't certain they believed that. When I worked for them, it was so I could pass easier through the world. A massive Minotaur was difficult to hide, although maybe at this point I could convince humans I was just a furry.

I thought about Paris and Ty. They were evil, evil bastards.

It was their fault Hercules had locked me up on that gods-forsaken island to begin with.

The old demigods were a problem. Theseus and Orpheus were the only ones left now, and they were holding onto their lives with everything they could. I knew what it felt like to watch others like you be killed, snuffed out by circumstance or hunted to extinction.

One thing I'd learned over the centuries—when the Fates said it was time, it was time.

I licked the icing off my fingertips as the driver weaved in and out of traffic. He was pretty talented. I had to give it to him, especially during morning rush hour.

Mentally, I went over the meeting again in my mind. There would be discussions about moving a couple of boundaries in the city to make things easier. And the twins supposedly had something they wanted to discuss, which made me anxious. I knew they would try to push me out of those decisions, too.

Perks of being a Minotaur—my bull-headedness went to another level. They wouldn't make me budge.

I'd tried to be pleasant to them, but the tensions between us seemed to only grow higher. I wasn't sure what to do about it, except monitor my businesses closely.

Both Damon and Ian seemed to think they were planning something. Not against me specifically, but something that might affect all of us. I didn't like them. I didn't trust them, either.

Maybe I was being paranoid.

The driver merged onto the highway. "We're about ten minutes out—"

BAM!

Glass exploded. Blood sprayed everywhere, metal crunching as the entire vehicle rocked as something slammed into the front. The front part caved in from the impact, the entire world ripped in half.

My ears buzzed as silence followed, interrupted by beeping and honking. Silver smoke twisted through the cabin.

I leaned forward and put my hand on the driver's shoulder—

"Damn it," I whispered.

He was dead.

I blinked as more smoke filled the cabin. Specks of blood covered my suit, and the last of my latte spilled over the seat and floor. I glanced over at my other guard, but he had passed out. Some of the glass had cut him, but I could hear his heart beating. I leaned over and unbuckled him, pulling him into my arms.

I shoved at my door. It fought me but then creaked, giving way to my strength. I dragged my guard out onto the road, and then off onto the side, out of the way, before rushing back to my totaled vehicle.

"What the fuck? How fucking far did you fall?" I mumbled.

Humans screamed in their cars, but for once in my long, monstrous life—they weren't screaming at me.

They were screaming at the body that had just fallen from the overpass above.

I craned my head back, staring at the overpass above us.

The sun had risen now, creating an unpleasant glare. I raised my brows, surprised to see two creatures peering over the edge. They reminded me of hell hounds, but not quite. They weren't like Cerberus, and they didn't feel the way other monsters did.

Their voices rattled through my mind, a metallic sound that made my skin crawl. *Give him to us, Minoan Bull.*

"Get the fuck out of here, beasts," I snarled. "This is my city. You aren't welcome here."

They snarled at me, but drew back regardless. I heard a lone howl, a sound of retreat.

Interesting.

I walked around to the front of the car, expecting to see a mangled body.

Instead, the man was in perfect shape.

There wasn't a single cut on him, not a single drop of blood that was his.

All my instincts ignited. I recognized *that* scent.

I knew their aura, the same as the countless others I had encountered over the years.

A fucking demigod just dropped on my car from the sky.

Either the gods were playing a joke on me or...

The brand on my throat burned, a reminder that I couldn't just kill him like I might have any other demigod. One of his hands twitched, his eyes fluttering.

I scowled. He was familiar, but I was certain we'd never met. Right? I would have known if I met a demigod.

He was too tall for me to carry in human form.

I cursed under my breath and pulled out my phone, dialing Damon's number. I hated calling him like this, but I at least knew he would answer. Having a friendship with someone after so long being alone was new to me.

I needed to get the demigod off the car, off the road, and somewhere out of sight from other monsters.

"Ryan. Where are you?" Damon answered gruffly.

"Ran into some problems. I won't be there."

The demigod on my car groaned. He raised his head for a moment, and then it fell back again.

"This meeting is important—"

"I know that. A man has fallen from the sky onto my car, but he's still alive."

"And? Leave him," Damon growled. "It's not like—"

"He's a demigod."

Damon was silent. He cleared his throat. "Well. I see. We understand. I hope you feel better, Ryan," he said, clearing his throat. "Sounds like a terrible sickness."

"Yes, terrible," I snorted, wondering who was hovering around him.

"We'll postpone this meeting and reschedule once you feel better."

"*Oh, for fuck's sake. Do monsters even get sick?*" I heard Orpheus snarl in the background.

I was about to hang up, but then a series of growls and snarls echoed in the room's background, followed by shouting. Another voice replaced Damons.

"Sick or not, it is a mandatory meeting. We have a way we do things around here."

Theseus.

I loathed him.

The hair on the back of my neck bristled, my muscles tightening. "I will not be at the meeting today. I am not well, as I told Damon."

The shouting continued in the background.

"You think you're better than us, but you'll regret this, Ryan. Remember that."

An explosion of voices echoed in the background and I hung up abruptly, smoke curling from my nostrils. Damon would not have taken kindly to that interruption. Maybe Theseus wouldn't be at the next meeting.

Nothing was going to plan. That irritated me, but I couldn't just bring this man with me. A fucking demigod had landed on my car like a cursed gift from the twisted gods.

Or even worse, a gift from the Fates.

For once, I was given something that could be used as an advantage. I felt like Theseus and Orpheus would do anything to get their hands on a new demigod so they could teach them to hate monsters. That would be a terrible thing.

I rolled my neck and let Theseus's warning roll off my back. He always said things like that. There were treaties in place that would prevent him from doing something too out of line.

The Fates wouldn't take kindly to him killing me after they'd just chosen me, right?

The man moaned again.

The worst part about helping this poor bastard out was ruining this suit.

I shed the mortal form the Fates gifted me, and it was like popping a can of biscuits. I growled as my bones and muscles snapped, everything burning with a searing, agonizing pain. With the pain came relief, though, the feeling of being myself. I grew taller and wider, my golden horns weighing down my head.

I should kill him.

I was ingrained with the temptation. It didn't matter that I was becoming friends with the demigods, Serena and Ashely. It didn't matter that I knew not all of them were bad. I was a monster created to hunt their kind, as I had for centuries.

The Fates were undoubtedly testing me.

"It's your lucky day, demigod," I growled. "You're coming home with me."

I picked him up, looking down at him. In my monster form, he felt fragile, even for an arguably large man.

Familiar. Why is he familiar?

There weren't supposed to be more demigods, and yet it seemed like they were coming out of the woodworks now. The gods had clearly forsaken whatever pact they'd made not to procreate, which was no surprise to me. Some things never changed.

Fire erupted on the hood of the car, black smoke curling into the air. I wasn't sure what the humans saw as I took off, my hooves clacking over the asphalt as I carried him off. All I knew was that they steered clear of us. Some took photos, others took videos, and to other people, it was just another day in Moirai City.

The journey back to one of my apartments was quick. For once, stifling traffic worked to our benefit.

I was furious my driver died, but that impact would have killed him, regardless. He was a mortal, and they were frail at best.

I wasn't sure what happened to the guard, either. He'd either show up or not. If he did, I probably owed him a raise...

Panic settled over me as I worried about my competence. Maybe I didn't know how to run things. I was supposed to inspire loyalty with my men, and all I could think to do most of the time was grunt at them. It wasn't like I even needed a guard as the Minoan Bull, but I got lonely sometimes. Really, the guards were around to explain things to me if I needed help. Like how social media worked.

It wasn't like there was a handbook for being the ultimate mafia Minotaur.

The man let out a sigh, but I tightened my grip around him as I went through the lobby doors. I ignored any looks that I got as I went to the elevator and jammed the button, shaking my head.

Of course, the first day of trying to be a real mafia boss was the day the Fates threw a damn demigod at me.

The door slid open. The elevator music was supposed to be smooth and relaxing, but it grated on my nerves as we rode up. It slowed to a stop on the wrong floor.

They slid open again, and I snarled, scaring the man standing there so badly he pissed himself. The doors shut again, finally taking me up to the right floor.

One of my guards was standing there. His eyes widened. "Uh..."

"Don't ask," I growled. "My car was ruined on the highway. Get Jeff to see if anyone else lived."

"Yes, sir..."

"Don't disturb us, no matter what you might hear."

"Uh...yes, sir."

I entered my apartment, tossed the demigod on the couch, and went to the whisky cabinet as my body shifted back into a human. It hurt like a motherfucker to shift, but it was worth it.

I rolled my shoulders and looked down at my body, realizing that my cock was hard.

The scent of the demigod hit me again, a mix that made my mouth water. I scowled at him.

I needed that whisky more now than ever before.

Chapter 3

The Naked Mafia Boss

rim

Dying was supposed to be a once in a lifetime event, but apparently not for me.

As I forced my eyes open, I knew I had died, even though I was alive again.

I had been in another place.

Another world...

I shivered. I didn't want to go back there. It was dark and creepy and confusing. I couldn't remember everything about it, but I knew that I wasn't supposed to be there. At least not yet. My thoughts lingered on that place for a few more moments before I shoved them away, trying to focus on the present.

I was alive. Lucky me.

My muscles ached, but otherwise I could move. The last

thing I remembered was flying off the overpass and then darkness.

I didn't know where I was. I forced my eyes open and stared at the ceiling, which was made of large black tiles. The couch I laid on was nice leather, too. I took a moment to feel it with my fingertips, feeling a tinge of jealousy. Someone rich had saved me.

The sound of glass clinking made me turn my head, looking across the living room.

I squinted. *What the actual fuck?*

I could only take so much strangeness in one day.

A naked man stood there guzzling whisky from the bottle. An actual ray of fucking sunshine filtered through the windows, highlighting his tan ass like a damn neon sign.

A nice ass, too.

Nice back muscles...

I pressed my lips together, drinking him in. It didn't hurt to look, even if he was my captor. Or savior. I wasn't sure yet.

"If this is some sort of sex cult, I don't want in," I croaked.

The naked man turned around, his eyes flashing a brilliant orange and red. I wasn't hallucinating, right? I'd really just seen the fire in his eyes.

His cock was hard and pierced and...

Fuck. This man was enormous.

I stared at him, the back of my mind rippling with fragments of a memory. He was familiar, even if I didn't recognize him immediately.

"Okay, I might be interested," I grunted.

"If you knew what I really looked like, I doubt you'd say the same thing." His voice was deep and rough. He lifted the bottle of whisky and poured some into a shot glass. He crossed the apartment to me and handed me the shot, his cock only inches from my face. "Drink."

I licked my lips and played along.

"Yes, sir," I muttered, grabbing the glass.

I downed the whole thing, completely bewildered as I tried to remember where I'd seen him before. He felt too familiar to be a complete stranger. There'd been a night a few months ago where I'd been with someone at a club, and I swore that someone was a monster, but...

When I woke up, I'd remembered little. The entire night was just a blur, from the beginning to end.

But his cock...

Even in the darkness of a sex club, I'd remember that cock.

Probably taking a drink from him was a stupid idea, but the entire day already defied logic. Getting drugged by a past one-night stand seemed unlikely.

"I don't really know what to do with you," he sighed, shrugging his shoulders. He looked down at me, his gaze simmering with molten heat, making me feel a lot of inappropriate things. Was this what Stockholm syndrome was like? "I should kill you, honestly. You ruined my car and killed my driver when you fell. But, I can't really kill demigods anymore..."

He said that so casually, my blood cooled. I shook my head. "I don't know what you're talking about, man. Demigods?"

He raised a blond brow. A faint silver scar slashed through it. "You're telling me you've had a normal life? Is falling from the sky just an average Monday for you?"

"Not at all," I croaked, holding out my shot glass. The corner of his mouth almost tugged into a smile as he poured me another. "Today has been..."

Today was shit.

"I doubt you'd believe me," I said, downing it. I studied him up and down, trying not to linger too long on his cock. "Have we met before?"

He took the glass from me and retreated to a black leather chair, plopping down on it.

His cock was *still* hard.

He didn't answer me, but the way he studied me, I knew he wondered the same.

"Are you...is there a reason that you're naked?" I asked.

He snorted. I could have sworn smoke curled out of his nostrils.

I slowly sat up, my muscles aching. Even my clothing seemed to be unscathed, which was bizarre considering how far I'd fallen. I rubbed the back of my neck, the tension making me sigh.

"Do you want the truth?" he finally asked.

"Sure. Might as well," I muttered.

"I'm a monster. You're a demigod."

Memories of a Minotaur flashed through my mind. Golden horns and smoke and hours of fucking in a dark backroom...

"You fell on my car in the middle of rush hour traffic. I carried you back to my apartment in my monster form, skipping a very important meeting, and against every instinct, I have let you live."

I scowled. I didn't like the way he said that.

"So now you're my problem until the Fates say otherwise."

"I'm not your problem," I said. "I don't plan on staying here. The police are out for me already. And I have a hard time believing you carried me back. I'm a big guy."

"I'll tell them to call off the search. Carrying you back here was one of the easiest things I've done this week. As I said, I am a monster. You are a demigod."

I stared at him and then let out a short laugh, not believing him. "What? You'll just 'call them off'?"

"Yeah. Easy. Did you already know that you're a demigod?"

I didn't answer him. How many times had I heard that

damn word today? First, it had been the talking head. Then the crow. Now him. Calling me a demigod—the way he said it, it felt like a curse.

"This morning, strange things happened," I said, shrugging them off. What was a Monday without a decapitation and life ending chase? "I don't know what being a demigod means. Like...one of my parents is a god?"

"Yes. Lucky you."

Who the hell was this guy? We continued to study each other as he took another sip of whisky. I couldn't help but look at his cock again. There were a thousand things I should have been thinking about right now, and the only one I could focus on was that night at the club.

"So you're hard because...?"

He shrugged. "Your scent appeases me. Clearly."

"Clearly," I mimicked.

He cocked his head. "Do you want to know what I really look like? Since you're *clearly* not believing what I'm saying. It might help us skip any of the bullshit."

"It's not that I don't believe you...but none of this is very believable. Then again, I was chased by monsters earlier. And then I fell off a bridge and I'm somehow still alive." *And I swear to the alleged gods that I remember you.*

His body reminded me of a chiseled statue as he stood. His eyes turned molten, his skin shimmering. My mouth fell open as he changed. The sound of bones crunching clapped through the luxurious apartment. Horns grew above his bullish head, gleaming in the sunlight. His muscles snapped, giving way to a larger body covered with dark, fine fur.

Holy fuck.

The bastard wasn't lying. He was a Minotaur.

I should have been scared. Earlier, the monsters that hunted me made me feel scared. But not him.

More memories flooded and my throat felt dry. I remembered his touch and the heat of his body against mine.

"You really are a Minotaur..."

"Not just any Minotaur. The Minoan Bull."

Smoke puffed from his nostrils.

My eyes moved down to his cock, and my mouth fell open again. He was massive—thick and long, with a bulbous tip and balls that made my mouth water. A bull ring pierced the head, golden just like his horns. Precum dripped from the tip, and it... it was also golden.

Being a monster fucker was apparently ingrained into me, because my cock hardened at the sight of him.

This was definitely him.

He let out a low laugh. "Does my monstrous form really please you?"

"Apparently." I wanted to ask him about that night and why I was just now remembering, but decided...if he didn't remember me either, maybe it was for the best. "I want you."

I wasn't sure I'd ever been so blunt before.

"I've had a bad day," I said. "I wouldn't mind working off some steam..."

He grunted, but came closer to me. It was difficult to peel my eyes off his cock, but I made myself look up.

"If I fucked you, you wouldn't be able to walk tomorrow," he whispered. "And it's the last thing either of us should do or even discuss."

"And? Didn't you say I'm your problem for now?"

I still didn't even know his name. He didn't know mine. I didn't even care.

We'd have one more memorable night, I'd sneak out, and escape to another city. And then, I would make sure to never see him again. Ever.

That would be the end. That would be it. No strings attached.

"One night," I offered. "If you want. Then I'll leave and you won't have to deal with me. I shouldn't actually be your problem, right? I don't want whatever this mess is. I'll get out of the city."

"If you really want me to fuck you, then get on your knees and beg."

My brows drew together. "Really?"

"Yes."

I swallowed hard.

The day I found out I was supposedly a demigod was going to be the same day I begged a Minotaur to fuck me. *Again.* If the Fates were real, they had a fucked up sense of humor.

Suddenly, nothing else really mattered. It had been too long since I'd been with someone, and the lust gripping me would not let go until I had my fill. I held his fiery gaze as I slid to the floor on my knees, his cock right in front of my lips.

"Please fuck me," I said. "I'm begging you."

His hand was massive as he gripped my chin. He curled his fingers into my dark beard, letting out a deep, guttural growl.

"Please," I whispered. "Just one night. Unless you don't want me."

"If I didn't want you, I wouldn't tell you to get on your knees," he said.

For a moment, his voice was a little softer, a little kinder. He tightened his grip and unhinged my jaw, offering me the head of his massive cock. It would be a Herculean feat to fit that in my mouth, but I would give it my best shot.

I bit the ring and tugged gently.

He grunted, his head falling back. *"Fuck."*

I smirked and traced the head with my tongue, reaching up

to cup his balls. They were heavy in my palms, full and ready. I kissed down his shaft, mentally counting the inches.

There were at least eleven. I'd seen toys this big before, but never anything in real life.

I took one of his balls and sucked gently.

"Gods damn it," he snarled. "You're fucking good at this."

I rolled it in my mouth and then traced the piercings on the underside of his cock with my tongue. I worked my way back to the tip, noting the gold dripping there.

The taste of his precum met my tongue, and I gasped, reeling as every nerve ending in my body lit up.

"What the hell?" I whispered.

I needed more of him. I licked it up, wishing he'd come so I could drink from him. I was bewildered, but I didn't want to stop. I sucked the head, swirling my tongue and listening to his erotic groans.

There was something powerful about making a monster like him make such sounds.

Really, this was going to be the highlight of the month. Maybe year.

I opened my mouth as wide as I could, attempting to take him. He looked down with a dark chuckle, sliding his hands to the sides of my head.

"You're an eager little monster fucker, aren't you?" he whispered. "Open wide."

He rammed forward, forcing it in. I groaned around him, the intrusion sending a shockwave through my body. My cock throbbed, begging for attention as he crammed his cock deeper, hitting the back of my throat.

Mentally, I came to terms with the fact that I was giving a blow-job to a monster.

And I fucking liked it.

He pulled back and then shoved forward again. The feeling

of being used made every muscle in my body relax. I relished it. I enjoyed giving control to him, even if we'd just met.

My eyes rolled back. He held me in place, more precum dripping down my throat. He pounded in and out slowly, fucking me at a speed that pulled me to the edge. Every thrust was full of intention.

I reached down and felt for my belt buckle. I undid it quickly, undoing my pants and letting my cock free. I needed to release so badly. The taste of his cum did something to me, setting off some sort of primal response that I couldn't control.

I stroked myself, moaning as he kept going.

"I'm going to breed you for hours," he huffed. "Do you understand me?"

I nodded, grunting around his cock. My jaw stretched, and I felt a burning sensation as the muscles were forced to remain open.

He fucked me harder, hitting the back of my throat strongly enough that I choked around him.

"When I'm done with you, you'll never want to fuck another," he snarled. "We're not doing this here, though. The walls are thin. We'll go to my estate where there's a forest."

He drew his hips back, pulling his cock free. I gasped, licking my lips. He leaned down, his face close to mine.

"I'm going to hunt you," he whispered. "And then I'm going to claim you."

"Are you sure you don't want to now?" I rasped. "We're both already on the edge."

"Yes. I'm certain. It would be easier to send you away from there too, considering you said you're wanted by the police."

I felt a sense of disappointment, but only because my body demanded we have sex now. He chuckled, his gaze sliding down.

"Put it away. And I'll have them get the chopper ready since you wrecked my car. We'll be there within the hour."

I shook my head. He was so casual about having a helicopter at his disposal. "Are you like a CEO or something?" I asked as I shoved my cock back into my pants. "Or just a rich dude with a secret?"

He pulled me to standing as he shifted back into his human form.

I realized I preferred the monstrous one.

"I'm a mafia boss," he said. "The Three Fates Mafia. We rule this city."

I wanted to laugh at how ominous, but also silly, that sounded. I wasn't sure if I was supposed to know what the Three Fates Mafia was, but I didn't care. That was the least of my concerns or worries after today.

"Alright. I'm ready to go when you are," I said. "You have lube at your house, right?"

"Plenty of it," he said. "Believe me. We'll make it fit."

Chapter 4

Hunt

Ryan

My helicopter lifted into the sky and the demigod next to me practically bounced up and down in his seat like some kid at an amusement park. I felt the urge to hold him in place every time he leaned over and pressed his face to the window.

"This is insane!" he hollered.

The first time I rode on one of these, it had been so Paris and Ty could flaunt their wealth. I had felt no sort of joy. But seeing his excitement made me smile.

I studied him, trying not to think about my sexy plans. He'd begged for my cock and agreed to a hunt. His eagerness to take part unearthed my sexual desires and fantasies.

I couldn't remember the last time I'd hunted someone for pleasure. It fulfilled a dark, primal part of me, pleasing the beast within. I would chase him down and fuck him so hard he'd beg for more.

My imagination was vivid. I closed my eyes for a moment, breathing in his addicting scent.

It had to be because he was a demigod. They always smelled good, even if he smelled infinitely better. Enough that my mouth kept watering.

My hands tightened into fists. I looked out the other window, focusing on the rattling of the chopper and not on the idea of fucking him here and now.

Of course, nothing was stopping me...

Fuck.

My cock throbbed. He looked over at me and smiled, and then his gaze slid down.

He raised a brow and slid closer.

My muscles tensed, but all I could do was nod.

He held up his hand and wiggled his fingers. "So they can't see," he said, gesturing to the guards.

I nodded, needing his hand on me.

I wanted more, but I wouldn't fuck him here.

I wanted to fuck him in my monstrous form, not this human condom I wore.

But...

He unbuckled my suit pants and pulled down the zipper, slipping his hand inside. His palm was warm against my erect cock, which throbbed in his warm grip.

He pulled it out and stroked me, his gaze flickering with mischief.

Fuck.

Today was going to be interesting.

He leaned over and spat on my cock, using his saliva to stroke me faster.

"Fuck," I growled.

"Do you want me to stop?"

My gaze flittered to the front of the helicopter. My pilot and guard at least knew not to look back.

Still...

"Don't stop," I growled.

He nodded and kept stroking. He held my gaze. The corner of his mouth tugged in a playful smirk.

My head fell back in pleasure and right as I came to the edge, he stopped.

I glowered at him as he tucked my cock away and winked. "More for later, right?"

"You're a bastard," I muttered, straining against my pants.

He only laughed.

Oh yeah, I was going to fuck him for hours.

The flight to the house didn't take much longer, nor did telling my guards to leave the premises. They were reluctant to, but a few growls sent them on their way. They would return tomorrow morning.

Finally, I had the demigod all to myself.

It had been a long time since I'd felt such potent desire. I was going to spend the next few hours fucking him, and then I was going to make sure he left the city.

The last thing we needed was another questionable demigod. The best scenario was I told Damon he actually died. That would be easier than alerting the entire mafia that another demigod had crash-landed in our laps.

There was something about him. He was familiar, but I couldn't quite place where. All I knew was that he didn't intend to hurt me and in this day and age, that was as good as you could get.

And if he did...

I'd killed demigods before. They were tough to incapacitate, but it could be done. And based on his reactions to the revelations, he didn't know what the hell he was. He didn't know what god he was spawned from.

I almost felt bad for him.

What I was doing with him was against my own rules I'd set long ago. But when I looked at him, the desire that curled through me was so potent, I couldn't simply walk away.

I needed to fuck him, get the lust out of my system, and then never see him again.

He stood on a balcony that overlooked the forest below. It was lunchtime, and mentally, I made a note to ask if he needed to eat.

"I haven't even asked your name," I said as I poured him a drink.

He turned around, and it hit me.

I knew exactly where I'd met him.

The club called The Labyrinth. Six months ago. I'd fucked a man and had shifted into a monster, but...

I felt a flash of rage and rushed towards him, pushing him towards the edge.

"What the fuck?" he growled, shoving against me.

I caged him against the balcony, smoke curling around us. "What the fuck is this, huh? Did someone send you to find me?"

"What are you talking about? You invited me here!"

"I remember *you*," I snarled. "From the club."

He rolled his eyes. "Yeah, I remember you too. Although I didn't initially because I actually don't recall much about that night. My memories are fuzzy, if you want to explain that."

I held his gaze, searching for the truth there. He seemed to be honest, although humans could be so difficult sometimes with their lies. The longer I stared at him, the longer I noticed little things that were bizarre. How the shadows seemed to find him, chasing away the sunlight even though it was midday. The golden flecks in his dark brown eyes, and how they shimmered with an otherworldliness that could only be attributed to a demigod, or even god.

When we first met, we'd both been in a dimly-lit club and drunk with lust. I felt that lust again now, but we couldn't hide from each other. I'd left that night wondering how a human could have taken me. I was a fool. I should have realized that he wasn't human.

I'd drugged him, hoping he would forget the monster part.

Clearly, that hadn't really worked.

Why had the Fates brought him to me again?

"I gave you something to make you forget because I thought you were just a human. I should have realized that you weren't." I stepped back, giving him room to breathe.

"I shouldn't be here," he muttered. He scowled and crossed his arms. "One night only. And my name is Grim."

A fitting name, it seemed. "You can call me Ryan," I said.

He snorted. "Ryan? The infamous ancient Minoan Bull is named Ryan?"

My jaw stiffened. "What's wrong with it? I picked it out. I like it."

He gave me a goofy smile and shrugged. "There's nothing wrong with it. I just expected something more menacing, I guess."

I let out a soft growl and mirrored his shrug.

"Ryan," he said softly again. "I mean, I like it."

I looked past him to the forest below, a deep ache distracting me momentarily. Now that I knew where I'd met him, it only made me want him more. That night was an unforgettable one. Even thinking about it, my cock throbbed in response, a primal craving for him.

I would hunt the demigod.

I would claim him and mark him and breed him.

And then I'd never see him again.

"You should eat before we hunt," I muttered.

"I'm not hungry," he said. "I'll eat after. I want you."

He stepped closer, and for the first time in centuries, I felt the flutter of nerves. It was a slight feeling that made me uneasy. Every part of my body wished to retreat and wished to stay still as Grim came closer. His hand was warm against my chest, felt through the silk shirt that I wore.

"Are you going to change back into a monster or not?"

I swallowed hard. "You are deeply unsettling," I muttered.

I couldn't understand why he didn't prefer me as a human. Still, his question alone unraveled me. He knew, too, and unbuttoned my shirt quickly. He pulled it free as my muscles grew and chuckled as he reached for my belt. He was quick and had me completely naked right as I changed, growing taller and releasing the beast within.

Grim was over six feet tall, and now he was a few feet shorter than me. He craned his head back and popped his lips, forming a silent *'wow'*.

"May I touch you?"

His voice was husky and soft. I nodded, unable to speak. I was a fucking mafia boss. A monster. And yet, I couldn't find the words as he slid his hands over my chest, circling my nipples. I shuddered, my head falling back.

"You're a witch," I mumbled as he felt me, hands roaming down to my hips.

His fingertips felt the edges there, grazing down to my cock. He gripped me gently, using both hands to hold my shaft. He felt the piercings underneath, letting out a satisfied hum as he stroked me.

"Grim," I whispered.

"Didn't they worship you back then?" he asked.

I shook my head, feeling a stab of pain in my chest.

"I would have."

I felt his lips wrap round the head of my cock and looked down to see him kneeling. Fuck.

I grabbed his dark hair, ruffling it as I held him in place. He moaned as I thrust forward, forcing more of my cock into him. I could feel the back of his throat.

Part of me wished the gods could see us now. Part of me wondered who his parent was and if they knew he was fucking a monster.

He cupped my balls as he kept sucking, and I shuddered.

"No," I rasped, pulling back. My cock slipped free, and he licked his lips. "I want to hunt you, Grim. Get up."

There was a flash of defiance there, which was something I wanted to explore later. I pulled him to his feet and tipped his chin up.

"You don't need food or water or anything?"

"No. Not now," he said. "After."

"Is there anything I should know?"

"If you're going to fuck me with this thing, you better bring lube with you into the woods," he said, motioning to my cock.

I snorted, amused. "Fair enough. What else?"

"I like pain. I like being surprised. I like being forced into things and used. My only request is that we spend some time together after."

"I can do that," I said.

"Then hunt me, foul beast," he teased. "Fuck me like an absolute raving monster. Prove that I'm a demigod and can take you."

I growled loud enough that his eyes widened. I watched his instincts raise red flags, his body stilling.

"Are you certain you want this, little king?" I asked.

"Yes."

"Then run, Grim. Run faster than you ever have before. Run like you're going to die if I catch you."

He took a tentative step back. I growled again, a sharp rumbling noise that got him moving.

The bastard took a step back and jumped over the balcony. I felt a flash of fear and ran to the edge, leaning over to see that he'd landed with ease.

He let out a laugh. "I've never done that before!"

He then looked up, shot me the middle finger, and took off running.

"You son of a bitch," I whispered.

I watched as he took off down the trail, disappearing into the dark trees. I'd give him a head start. Every primal instinct told me to hunt *now*, but I would hold on until I could truly chase him. While I waited, I went back into the house, secured a bottle of lube, and wondered how I would bring it with me. I wasn't sure how frightening a massive Minotaur hunting you down while holding a bottle of lube was, but perhaps the intention would be enough.

I returned to the balcony and, like Grim, leapt over the edge. It didn't matter that it was two stories in the air. I landed with ease, my senses roaring to life. His scent was like a tracker. I paced back and forth, counting in my head. The minutes passed quickly.

It was time to hunt.

The wind picked up, giving me his scent. It was a mixture of evergreen, oakmoss, and leather. I drank it in, groaning as pleasure bloomed through me. I could feel the need in my veins, a desire that must be satiated.

I let out a bellow.

Birds erupted from the trees, scattering into the sky as they knew there was a monster in their forest. My hooves dug into the ground and I took off running, lumbering down the path in the same direction Grim took.

My instincts lead me. I ran down the path until I noticed broken branches, and veered to the left, bursting through the trees. They crunched and snapped, growing in a thick mass that was difficult to break through.

He was using my size to his advantage.

I let out a satisfied chuckle and pushed through, breaking past them. The brush cleared up, his scent growing stronger.

I knew there was a part of him that was scared. He should have been scared. I was a monster hunting him down, ready to use him however I saw fit.

Perhaps it wasn't wise on his part that he told me he liked pain.

I gripped the lube bottle as I pushed through more trees, finding the path he'd taken. I burst out onto the worn path and paused, looking behind me. I could see the house from here.

He was clever. He'd lead me in a circle.

"Smart little king," I said, lifting my nose to the breeze again. "And stupid too."

I had him.

This was my favorite part of the hunt.

The moment right before the true chase.

I took off down the path again, pushing faster. Harder. His scent came closer, taunting me.

"I've got you," I snarled.

I took a right and burst through two trees, reaching out to grab a jacket.

Only it was just a jacket.

Every muscle in my body now vibrated with frustration.

"When I find you, I'm going to fuck you until you're a begging mess," I snarled.

I heard a chuckle and looked up.

Clinging to the trunk up in the air and seated on a large branch was Grim. He met my angry gaze with a grin that nearly made me melt.

"Is this cheating?" he taunted.

I tossed the bottle of lube on the ground and rolled my shoulders.

A tree could come down. And he was a demigod. He certainly wouldn't die.

I saw that fact dawn on Grim.

"Surely not," he called down.

I took a few steps back, positioned my horns and top of my head for the trunk.

"I'm bull-headed," I said. "Even you should have realized that by now."

I heard his laugh as I lunged forward, ramming into the tree vigorously enough some of the bark cracked.

It would take some work to bring it down, but the prize was worth it.

Chapter 5

Railed by the Minotaur

Grim

My plan to climb up a tree and hide in it was brilliant. Only, I hadn't factored in the fact that Ryan was very strong, and that it wouldn't take him long to bring down an entire fucking tree. The trunk trembled as he rammed into it again, the sound of wood snapping echoing through the forest.

Watching him go through all this effort just to get to me made me hard. I sucked in a breath, sliding my hand over my cock through my pants. His muscles rippled with unnatural strength, his strenuous grunting music to my ears.

I'd let go of wondering if there was something wrong with me. I didn't care that he was a monster. I remembered bits and pieces of that night at the club. Even if he'd drugged me to forget, one didn't simply forget fucking a Minotaur with a pierced cock.

We'd get this out of our system and I'd disappear into the dawn, leaving Moirai for good.

Ryan rammed into the tree again and it snapped more. I felt the ominous moment, a silence before a series of cracks followed, louder than before as wood split.

Fuck.

He'd done it.

Fear held me in place as the tree wavered. I'd fallen from the overpass and lived, so surely this wouldn't be an issue, right? I cursed under my breath and then let go, falling through the air.

A set of muscled arms caught me.

The tree crashed into other trees, the sound of it falling unlike anything I'd ever heard. The ground rumbled beneath us and I tensed, closing my eyes as it crashed.

"Mine," he snarled.

I plopped to the ground. My eyes flew open as he pinned me beneath him, his massive body pressed into mine. He grabbed my shirt and ripped with ease, splitting the fabric and baring my chest. My cock pulsed, pressing against my pants as he freed me from my clothing. Within a few moments, I was completely naked and aware of the fact that I was giving myself to him.

The release settled over me. It wasn't very often that I could trust someone, but I trusted him. My breath hitched as he gripped my cock, clasping it firmly.

"Beg," he snarled.

"Fuck," I rasped. I stared up at him, taking in his fiery eyes and gleaming horns. His shoulders were twice as broad as mine, his body covered in a soft down of dark fur.

I wanted him. I wanted him so severely that I couldn't think of anything else but him. My cock throbbed in his grip, which tightened enough to make me huff.

"Please," I rasped. "Please fuck me. I want to feel like I did that night."

"At the mercy of a monster," he snarled, squeezing harder.

I cried out, bucking beneath him. "Please!" This time, my plea was genuine. I gasped as he released my cock and grabbed my neck, squeezing the sides and cutting off my breath.

Being choked by him made me feel alive. My blood rushed and I could hear it, my heart pounding faster and louder. I tried to drag in a breath, but he wouldn't let me. He held me in place as his other hand slid down my body, pushing my legs back.

"Hold them in place," he commanded.

I held the backs of my thighs, my body blaring with alarms because he had yet to let me breathe.

"Struggle against me and everything stops, little king."

Fuck. I liked that pet name.

My lungs burned, my instincts begging me for air. I made a choking sound, but he didn't relent. Instead, he rubbed his cock against mine, the size difference between us turning me on.

Maybe coming out in the woods with a stranger had been a mistake.

He chuckled and eased his grip on my throat. I dragged in several breaths, panting as a euphoric rush flooded me. My head spun as he leaned back, grabbing the bottle of lube. He uncapped it and spread a generous amount over his cock and then dripped some on my cock and hole. I whimpered as he worked it over my body, using two massive fingers to tease and prod.

"You're such an eager slut," he whispered. "You're going to take every inch of my cock. Every fucking inch. Do you understand?"

I nodded and moaned as he pushed two fingers inside of me, stretching me around them. Every piece of resistance shattered as I gave into him. I didn't care if I begged, cried, whimpered. Every sound I made was desperate and hungry. I was greedy for his touch.

"Fuck me," I rasped. "Please. I need to feel you inside of me."

I pulled my legs back further as he slipped a third finger inside of me. "You're too fucking tight," he growled.

There was a bit of pain as he worked me energetically, but it didn't take long until all I felt was pleasure. His fingertips pressed against my prostate, and my cock was painfully hard. Precum beaded, dripping down the head.

My eyes fluttered, a long groan leaving me. He thrust them in and out and then pulled back, replacing his fingers with the head of his massive cock. I looked down between us, wondering how the hell I'd taken him the first time. Even some of the largest fantasy dildos I'd seen were smaller and less intimidating.

"Take a deep breath," he whispered.

His softness made me whimper. I did as he asked and drew in a deep breath.

He pumped forward, giving me the first couple of inches. I stretched around him and grunted, my fingertips digging into my thighs. He wore a satisfied expression as he gave me more, pushing inside of me until I'd taken half his cock.

"Fuck," I groaned. "*Fuck.*"

He moaned, his body shivering. "You're so tight. You're milking my cock."

All I could do was nod. I bit my lower lip, forcing myself to breathe and relax, and he pulled back and then shoved forward again. He leaned down, and I parted my lips, accepting his monstrous kiss. He devoured me, our tongues thrashing against each other as he fucked me.

Every movement was tortuous and wonderful. I could feel the leaves and sticks digging into my back, but that didn't matter. He pounded more powerfully this time, nearly filling me to the hilt. My shout echoed around us and he chuckled as he pulled back and did it again.

"I'm just getting you used to it," he whispered.

I shivered as he drove in and out. He was being gentle, I realized. I released my legs and wrapped them around his hips as best as I could, winding my arms around his thick neck.

"Harder," I begged.

He growled, but did as I asked, jackhammering into me hard enough that I screamed again. He snarled as he drove in and out, his cock going deeper and deeper. I felt like I was being impaled, his cock branding my insides.

"*Please*," I moaned.

"Please what?"

"Harder. Faster. *More*."

I grunted as he went harder and faster, the sound of his balls slapping against me turning me on even more than before. I gasped as he gripped my cock and stroked, a low rumble in his chest.

"You're going to be crawling out of this fucking city," he rasped.

He kept the strokes at the right pressure, even as he plunged in and out. He growled, his hips bucking with another thrust.

I felt a sense of awe watching him come. Heat splashed inside of me, burning me from the inside out. Branding me, breeding me. The rush of it all made me come too. I arched against him, crying out as I orgasmed.

He groaned, going still as more of his cum flooded me. He held his hand to his mouth, licking up the mess I made. His nostrils flared, his cock still pushing more into me.

"There's so much," I whispered.

The more he filled me, the more I could feel my muscles

relaxing. His seed was like a drug, preparing me for more. And I wanted more. I wanted to be like this for hours, taking his monstrous cock.

He shuddered as he delivered the last load.

I melted against the ground, out of breath. He planted his hands on either side of my head and sighed, his muscles finally relaxing.

"You're clever, you know?" he chuckled. "Leading me in a circle. Climbing the tree."

"Perhaps they're my supposed demigod instincts."

There was a hint of bitterness in my voice. He cocked his head, studying me.

"Did you really not know?" he asked softly.

I shook my head. This felt like a strange conversation to have while still full of him, but I spoke anyway. "No. The last few months have been...bizarre. Since we met the first time. Before then, my life was normal. For the most part."

"Hold still," he said.

He slowly eased back, pulling his cock free. I grunted as his cum gushed out of me. Before I could make a move, he scooped me up and carried me bridal style through the woods.

Today had to be the wildest day of my life. I stared up at him, wondering what tomorrow would be like.

He carried me silently back to the house, going through a set of double doors. The house was stunning. It was masculine and warm despite the cold exterior. The walls were painted black, and the hardwoods were dark mahogany.

"I can leave now," I said, feeling restless.

"We have the whole day and night. You didn't think you'd get off that easy, did you?"

"Well, you hunted me..."

He snorted. "Shut up, Grim."

"Okay," I mumbled.

I quieted as he carried me up a massive staircase to a spacious bedroom. The bed at the center was large enough to sleep a Minotaur and more. Black curtains blocked out any light, bathing us in cool darkness.

A bathroom joined the bedroom, dark marble with ribbons of gold and gray. I glanced around with wide eyes.

"I'm a mechanic," I blurted out.

"And?"

And? I felt out of place in this sort of bathroom. And he still didn't let me go, even as he stepped into a huge walk-in shower and pressed a button. A soft sound echoed and hot water started, steam curling around our bodies. He stepped under the shower head, the water running over us.

He didn't put me down, but he changed how he held me. In a swift move, he brought my legs around his hips, shoved me against the wall, and thrust up—filling me all over again.

I cried out, gasping.

"How are you still hard?" I moaned.

"I can go for hours, little king." He bounced me up and down slowly, giving and taking away his cock.

I raked my fingers down his chest, my head falling against the wall as hot water streamed down our bodies. I sank into the feeling of being taken again, the heat building between us. Over and over, he took me, until the water ran cold.

His touch gentled and he kissed me again, deeper than before. I realized I didn't want him to be gentle, because being gentle made me feel vulnerable. And feeling vulnerable after everything that happened...

He came inside me again with a long moan. I held onto him, blinking back tears and praying I could get whatever emotions I felt in check. He pressed his forehead to mine, breathing us in.

"You're unhappy," he whispered.

"It's complicated." My voice was husky and raw.

"You can tell me."

"I can't."

"You can. We'll never see each other again after tonight. You can tell me anything and everything." He dragged his cock out again, his seed dripping from me.

He put me down gently and grabbed a bar of soap, lathering it up and washing our bodies. I didn't fight him as he washed us, his hands firm and comforting.

"Hey," he said, tipping my chin up. "I mean it. Talk."

I held his gaze but then relented. "It would be better if you're not gentle or kind. Because it makes me feel vulnerable."

"It makes you feel cared for."

My jaw stiffened, and I nodded. He turned off the water and stepped out, handing me a fluffy navy towel that was soft and warm. I wrapped it around my body and watched as he grabbed one too.

"Why does it matter if someone cares for you? Don't you have friends or family?"

"Every person who I have cared for dies."

He scowled, giving me a look of disbelief. "Not everyone?"

"Every single person. I grew up without parents. Briefly raised by my grandparents. They died. Handed off to my aunt and uncle. They died. Handed off to a distant cousin. They died. Went into foster care and through several homes where someone died. Became an adult and at least once a year, I find a dead body. And then there's the last six months. Almost every week, I've found one. Just this morning I walked in on my decapitated boss. I am cursed."

I breathed out. I hadn't intended to say all of that, but clearly I'd needed to.

"You're a demigod," Ryan said, as if that explained it all.

"I don't know what being a demigod means. I know, in

theory, what it means, but I don't understand why it's important. I don't believe the gods are real."

"You've fucked an actual Minotaur twice, but you don't believe the gods are real?"

"If there are truly gods, then I hope they all die."

Ryan froze as the lights flickered in the bathroom. "He didn't mean it," he muttered. "You have every right to hate them, but you should still watch your tongue. Gods are fickle beings. And with you being a demigod, they're more likely to overhear you."

"Then I hope they hear me," I muttered. "And I hope they know I think they suck at their jobs."

Ryan stepped closer to me and tugged on the towel, bringing me close to his body. Heat radiated off him like a furnace. He tipped my chin up, tracing my bottom lip with his thumb.

"We met at a sex club," he said. "What kind of kinks do you have? Surely more than being hunted down and fucked by a monster."

It was a distraction, but it worked. We still had hours to play, and I needed to get every ounce of lust and frustration out of my system before returning to the real world. He kept my chin tilted as he stared down at me, so very gentle for a monster that just nearly railed me into the afterlife.

"I enjoy many things," I sighed. "Breath play. Being blindfolded and bound and taken. I think because I'm strong, I enjoy being made helpless."

He nodded. "What else? Tell me all your darkest secrets and desires."

I snorted and tugged my face away, but his grip tightened, holding me in place. Finally, I relented. "Ball gags, collars, harnesses, rope, leashes, muzzles, knives, spreader bars, cock worship, and nipple play all come to mind."

He laughed loud enough that it startled me. I raised a brow as he released me and turned, leaving the bathroom. Was I supposed to follow him? I pulled the towel around my shoulders and went after him.

"We don't have to use all..." I trailed off as he left the bedroom.

I scowled as I hurried after him, following him down the hall to a set of double doors. He pushed them open and stepped to the side, revealing a space that I truly envied.

"You have a dungeon," I said, looking around excitedly. "Is this where you bring all your boys?"

He let out a low chuckle and stepped up behind me, his cock nudging me. "No. But I have it because I enjoy things, and on the off chance I ever find someone that does as well, it's available. It's far easier to bring someone here, isn't it?"

I nodded as I took in the room. Like the rest of the house, it was masculine but warm. The walls were mirrors and reflected the two of us, and together, we were strange to behold. He slipped his hand around my throat, gripping gently.

Fuck.

The chemistry between us was undeniable. Once again, every worry and thought went blank from his touch. Maybe part of being a demigod was being able to perpetually recover, but my cock stiffened as he squeezed, and especially as he rocked his hips against my ass.

"I'm going to go downstairs and get you nourishment. While you wait, pick out what you want to use. Everything is sanitized."

He released me and retreated, leaving me alone in a state of horny bewilderment. I grunted and dropped the towel, going to a wall with racks of different toys. Some of them looked absolutely terrifying...and interesting.

I picked up a leather paddle with silver spikes, testing it on my thigh. I winced and my cock lengthened, the pain enjoyable.

Keeping that one. I held onto it as I continued to peruse, picking out a black leather harness that still smelled new. Fresh leather could be a kink of itself. A ball gag and muzzle, spreader bars, several knives.

He was right about me crawling to a different city tomorrow, but I didn't care. When in Rome, right?

Rustling sounded behind me and I spun around. Ryan stood in the doorway with a tray full of cheese, bread, vegetables, and meats. He also brought water.

My stomach fluttered again. I put a metal wall around the way it made me feel to be cared for, caging the emotions in. After tonight, we'd part, and the Minotaur would just be a memory.

Chapter 6

Dusk to Dawn

Ryan

While Grim finished eating and drinking, I looked over the items he'd chosen. My imagination went wild as my gaze roamed over them, formulating a plan of pleasure and pain.

There was a discrete clock on the wall. I glanced at it, making a mental note that we had fifteen hours to do whatever we wanted to do together. The sun rose around six A.M., which was when Grim would leave. I'd already decided that I'd send him off with a new motorcycle since his other one was wrecked.

Maybe I was being too caring. But it was hard not to do nice things when it had been so long since anyone had shown interest in me. I enjoyed pleasing him.

I rubbed the back of my bulky neck. Being in my full form

without being hated or judged made me relax in a way I hadn't in a long time.

"Thanks for the lunch."

I turned to look at Grim. He stretched out on the chaise, fully naked and looking comfortable. I admired him, wondering if...

He raised a brow. "Now, you have to tell me all your deepest, darkest desires. Since you haven't yet."

I snorted and shrugged. "I enjoy the things you do."

"And?"

I hesitated but then decided—fuck it. We'd said we'd do whatever we wanted tonight. He'd been vulnerable with me, the least I could do was return the favor.

"I like the idea of you fucking me. It's just that aside from doing things to myself..."

Both of his dark brows shot up, a smirk twisting his lips. "You want me to fuck you?"

"Yes."

"I'd love to."

"Okay," I breathed out. Why was it so easy to ask someone what they wanted and so damn difficult to say what I did? Centuries of living didn't make that easier.

Grim set up and put the tray and glass on a small table. He then knelt on the floor, which was softened by matts that were spongy and good for impact. My strength was less likely to actually harm a lover if they could land safely...

I picked up a blindfold and went to him. His complete submission pleased me, as did how easy-going he was. I had a feeling that was mostly a veneer, the result of someone who had seen too much in a brief span of years.

"Thank you," I whispered.

"For what?" he asked.

"For being with me." I raised the blindfold and covered his eyes, tying it around the back of his head.

"I don't know why you're thanking me for that," he mumbled.

When he scowled, it amused me. I didn't explain why I thanked him, instead leaving him kneeling there. The toys he chose were laid out on a sex bench, which I would soon be using.

His anticipation grew. That was my favorite part about enjoying things like this. Sex wasn't just penetration. The act of using someone in such a way brought me as much pleasure as breeding them. I cherished his submission and trust.

He let out a soft groan. I picked up the ball gag and muzzle and went to him. First, I fitted the ballgag around his head, forcing his mouth open.

His last word before I popped the ball in was fuck.

I tightened it and then put the muzzle around his head. The leather piece was held securely in place by four straps, three chrome buckles, and a collar that fit around his neck. By the time I finished securing everything, he couldn't see or speak.

"If this is too much, your safeword is a hand signal. Show me what it is."

He raised his right hand and formed a peace sign.

"Good," I said.

I ran my fingers through his hair and gripped, giving him a light tug. He groaned around the gag, his breath hitching.

I released him, knowing he wanted more. The tension in the room mounted as I moved around him, circling him like a shark that smelled blood in the water.

We had hours to play. And now, I would use that time to push him some.

I went to the chaise and sat down, sprawling out. My cock

was hard, which was no surprise. Seeing a sexy man on his knees, muzzled and blindfolded and waiting for me—that was beyond hot.

"Ry—ah—?"

I fought the urge to laugh as he tried to say my name. His breathing quickened for a moment and then...he completely relaxed. His back muscles softened, his heart calming. The soft beat was a metronome to me, easing as I gripped my shaft and stroked.

He had this effect on me that was almost unnatural. Maybe it was because he was a demigod, but he was driving me crazy.

My body shuddered as I stroked fast. I huffed, my head falling back as I masturbated to the obedient sight of him. Having his cock inside me later would be a new experience for me, one that I wanted so much.

"The sight of you pleases me," I grunted.

He nodded, letting out a low whimper.

I kept pistoning my cock, groaning as pleasure enveloped me. I came to the edge and stopped, my chest heaving with pants.

I wasn't ready to come yet.

I rose from the chaise and went to the bench, picking up the leash and spiked paddle. Grim made a soft noise as I went back to him and knelt behind him. I clipped the leash to his collar and gave him a strong shove to all fours. He caught himself with a groan, pushing his ass back against my cock.

"Fuck," I growled.

He knew how to tempt me. He pushed back, rubbing against me slowly. I didn't stop him from doing so. It took every ounce of control and willpower not to immediately ram into him and fill him, but I could hold myself in check.

I gripped the paddle and dragged the spikes on one side down his back. He shivered, his head dropping and shoulders raising like a cat. He smelled like my soap and musk. I reached down and grabbed his head, shoving him down so that his ass was raised in the air. His body was so small compared to mine, and I hovered over him, enjoying our size difference.

"You're so good," I whispered.

I leaned back on my haunches, admiring his ass. I flipped the paddle over, teasing him with the smooth side. I slapped his ass cheek with it, starting with light pressure until his skin bloomed red. I changed to the other cheek, working them both in tandem until I knew I could hit him harder.

The moment I truly spanked him, he shouted in pain, his voice echoing around the gag and through the room. If my men had been in the house, they might have come running. Part of me wished I would have kept them around just so they could barge in and see how perfect he looked right now.

"My little demigod whore," I said. "Count to five."

He tried his best, even though his words were gargled from the gag.

One.

I spanked him harder, the slap accompanied by a cry.

Two.

Again, I spanked him, using the flat side. It was powerful enough that if he were a human, he would have used his safeword. The pain was fierce enough that goosebumps erupted over his skin, his ass fire-engine red.

Three.

His entire body tensed, ready for another heavy blow. Instead, I flipped the paddle and lightly spanked him with the spikes. It surprised him, and that surprise pleased me.

Now, he didn't know which side I would use.

And that was part of the fun.

Messing with his mind, teasing his senses.

Four.

This time, I spanked him with the spiked side. He grunted, his body shivering as he took the pain. The spikes left sharp pin-pricks, needle like marks that were close to drawing blood.

I couldn't risk drawing a demigod's golden blood. I felt a pang of regret, because I wanted to go longer, but I flipped it back to the flat side.

Five.

I made the last spanking count. Grim cried out, his body arching as the paddle impacted him. Sweat blanketed his skin as he trembled.

I ran my palm over his ass, gently squeezing his cheeks. His flesh was hot to the touch, as if he'd been branded. He moaned as I caressed him. Reaching down, I took hold of the leash and pulled on it, putting him back into an all fours position.

My cock begged me to take him, and my will to resist finally crumbled. I fit the head of my cock between his ass cheeks, noting that he was still lubed up from my cum. He nodded, grunting as he pushed back.

He took the head of my cock, slipping around me like a vise. I growled, pulling on the leash and gripping his hip. I stayed still as he continued to work himself onto my cock, enjoying the control.

I kept the leash taut and thrust forward, filling him entirely. His muscles squeezed tight around me as he cried out. Euphoria clouded my mind, my balls aching to fill him with my seed.

He pushed back, riding my cock faster. I looked down, drinking in the sight of him. "You take me so well," I huffed.

Grim whimpered in response, pleasure rippling through his body. My head tilted back as I held onto the leash, reveling in the waves rolling through me.

I was so close.

I was so fucking close.

I'd lost track of how many times he'd made me come today, and I wasn't slowing down. I growled, my hips jerking as I came, pumping every drop inside of him.

My cock pulsed inside him as I opened my eyes. I reached down, unlatching the muzzle and ball-gag. They fell to the floor, and he breathed deep. I pulled off the blindfold last.

"Fuck," he rasped. "That was..."

"Glorious," I mumbled, driving deeper into him as the last of my seed spurted inside his hot hole.

Grim nodded and looked back at me over his shoulder. "When is it my turn?"

His tone was flirtatious, which made me smile. "I'm still balls deep inside of you and you want to know when—"

"I get to return the favor."

I pulled out of him slowly, my cum dripping to the floor in copious amounts. I sat back and raised a brow. "Clean this up and then you can fuck me. I'll be waiting in my bed."

"Yes, *Sir*," he whispered, his eyes burning with excitement.

* * *

It didn't take long for him to clean up. I waited on my bed, sprawled out and wondering what it would feel like for him to fuck me. I felt a mixture of nerves and anticipation, which was a new feeling after living for so long.

He was quiet as he entered my dark bedroom. I swallowed hard and looked back at him. He held the bottle of lube the same way I had earlier, like it was a threat. But it was a sexy threat.

"Surely, the powerful and great Minoan Bull is not nervous about being fucked by me," he teased as he knelt on the bed.

I didn't know what to say. Grim chuckled and reached for me, rolling me onto my back. He straddled my stomach and leaned down, kissing me fiercely.

The room was cool and safe. I breathed him in, accepting

the kisses he trailed down my chest, sliding lower until he came to kneel between my legs. He gripped my cock and hummed, stroking the velvety shaft before cupping my balls.

"Turn over," he whispered.

I did as he requested and repositioned myself, turning back over onto my stomach. He remained kneeling between my legs and ran his hands up the back of my thighs, kneading me slowly.

I relaxed, breathing in his comforting scent. It took a lot to trust him, but in this moment, I did. I gave into what I wanted, feeling him the way he did me.

He leaned down and parted my ass cheeks, still kissing me. I gasped as I felt the tip of his tongue rimming me, sending a bolt of pleasure through my body.

"*Fuuuck,*" I rasped, burying my head into a pillow.

He chuckled as he kept going, circling and teasing me. My cock throbbed, my fingers curling into the bedsheets.

I tensed as he leaned back, replacing his tongue with a fingertip.

"Relax," he whispered. "We both know you can take way more than this."

I almost told him to fuck off, but then he pushed another finger inside, and my thoughts evaporated. I grunted, sinking into the feeling of him teasing me. Pleasure rippled through me in soft waves as he explored, his patience humbling me.

"Grim," I rasped. "I want you inside me."

"Not yet."

His answer was firm and surprised me. I always made the decisions and took control during sex, but having someone else take the lead...

Every muscle in my body relaxed in response to him. It was like magic, his touch working a spell over me.

"Good boy," he whispered. "I can feel you relaxing for me. You'll take me soon, won't you?"

What the fuck?

I preened under his words, even if they shocked me. Everything that I knew about myself when it came to sex and kink tilted on its axis, leaving me wondering how far I'd go with him in control.

"Prop up on your knees," he said, patting my ass.

I did as he asked, getting into the same position I'd put him in earlier. My chest and head pressed into the bed, my ass up in the air and cock throbbing between my thighs.

He grabbed my cock with one hand and pushed a third finger inside of me, working them in tandem.

"Fuck," I snarled, moaning as he continued. "Grim, what are you doing to me?"

"Just pleasing you the same way you please me," he murmured, stroking me in long, methodical jerks.

I shivered as he continued, closing my eyes and letting the feelings wash over me. I felt vulnerable. And as a monster and mafia boss, that wasn't an emotion I enjoyed...until now.

"I can't wait to fuck you," he said. "My cock is so hard right now. And so is yours."

He teased the piercing around the head, giving it a slight tug. My breath hitched as he pulled his hand free and rose behind me, gripping my hips. I looked back at him over my shoulder, studying his expression and the way his eyes were lit with desire.

Grim *wanted* me.

He leaned over and grabbed the bottle of lube, pouring some on me and himself.

"Is this really your first time?" he asked.

"Yes."

He smirked. "So I'm popping your cherry, huh?"

"Shut up and fuck me, Grim."

He responded by pressing the head of his cock against me. I sucked in a breath but made myself relax as he thrust forward, filling me slowly. The two of us groaned together, his fingers digging into my muscles.

"Fuck," he huffed. "You feel so good."

All I could do was nod.

He drove deeper into me until he stopped, allowing me to stretch around him.

"You're doing well."

He pulled out slowly and then pushed back in, drawing another moan from me. I nodded, looking back at him.

"More," I rasped.

His hips jerked as he fell into a harsh rhythm that made me spiral. My eyes fluttered closed as he moved in and out, his cock filling me over and over again.

"Do you have a breeding kink?" he asked.

My cock immediately thickened to full length. I was breathless as I nodded, my mind reeling at the thought of him filling me.

Clearly, the answer was yes.

"I'm going to pump you full of my cum," he growled. "A monster fucked by a demigod."

"Fuck," I grunted.

His words made me shudder. I was close to coming again, even without my cock being stroked. Every slam of his cock made me feel like I was going to fall apart.

"More," I begged.

He groaned and pistoned into me with more force, repeatedly. I lost myself in his touch, in the feeling of being taken. He made me gasp and moan and beg, pushing me further and further.

"I'm so close," he said, reaching around to grip my cock.

"Fill me," I whimpered. "Please."

He gripped my cock at the same moment he shot inside, and the two of us came together. I cried out as hot cum spurted inside of me, all while I came from his touch too.

"Oh gods," I panted, collapsing beneath him.

He didn't pull out and leaned forward, his body draping over mine as we caught our breaths.

I wished the two of us could stay like this forever.

Chapter 7
Other Demigods Are Assholes

Grim

Like we promised each other, the moment the sun rose, I got dressed and ready to leave for good.

Ryan snored a little longer, but as I pulled on my shoes, his eyes opened and he watched me quietly.

"It's morning," I mumbled.

He sat up in bed, the blankets gathering around his waist. I tried not to focus on him or his muscles or anything else I found attractive about him as I went to the bedroom doorway.

"I'll walk you out," he said.

He got out of bed and stretched. He snapped his fingers, and the curtains in the room pulled back automatically, letting the dawn light in.

I wasn't sure how late we stayed up fucking each other. I was tired and sore, but happier than I'd felt in ages.

Happy and sad.

I didn't want to leave, but I couldn't stay.

Ryan followed me silently downstairs, his hooves clacking on the hardwoods. He grabbed a bag and a set of keys from a small table in the entryway and held them out for me.

"What's this?" I asked.

"They're for a motorcycle, since you wrecked yours. And the bag has money and a new ID in it. You can get out of Moirai and start over."

"When did you ever have time…"

"Made a call while you slept," he said with a shrug.

Like it was so simple.

I swallowed hard and shook my head. "I can't accept this. It's too much."

"You can and will. I have more than enough money, and after last night…Well, it's a way to say thank you. Just take it and go."

I stared and then nodded, snatching them from him. They felt heavy in my hands, an ache radiating through my chest.

He opened the front door for me, his gaze softening.

I'd never been so intimate with someone before, and I had a feeling he hadn't either. There'd been moments within the last twenty-four hours that shocked both of us.

"I know we said we'll never see each other, but…if you ever need help, find me. Okay?"

I forced myself to look at him, even if it would have been easier not to.

"You're a demigod, and I hate to say it, but trouble tends to find you."

"I know that," I mumbled.

He forced another smile. "You'll be okay."

It would have been easier to be cold too, but I couldn't find a shred of that within myself. "I will. Hopefully, things calm down."

His doubtful expression told me they wouldn't.

"This city is probably part of the problem," he said. "Too many monsters and demigods. That energy is bound to go after you. I'm sure once you're far away, you can live a more normal life. You don't want this."

He raised a black helmet up and fit it over my head, securing it. The motions made me blush, reminding me of the muzzle. Fuck. I would think about last night for a long time. He flipped the visor down, checked the jacket I wore, and nodded.

"Be safe, Grim."

"I will."

Well, I'd try.

I stepped out into the cool morning and slid my backpack on, annoyed by the signing birds in the trees. It was another sunrise and far too nice for the way I felt.

The motorcycle waited at the base of the marble stairs, sleek and expensive. I shook my head. I couldn't believe he'd just gifted this to me like it was nothing.

I went down the steps without looking back, got on the bike, and put the key in the ignition. I cranked it and it roared to life, interrupting the peaceful morning. Birds scattered into the scarlet sky.

I couldn't look back at him now.

Every muscle in my body ached for his touch, and that hurt. I was thankful that I'd forgotten most of our last encounter now, because I had a feeling I would have wanted to find him again.

The bike lurched forward as I rotated the throttle. I swore I heard him say *goodbye* as I took off.

I increased my speed as I merged on the road, letting my

instincts guide me. Moirai City was to the left, so I'd take a right.

Even though I could no longer see the house, I could still feel him. It wouldn't take long to shake that feeling, though. It wasn't like we really knew each other.

Fuck. I fought the emotions as I kept driving and even sped up, as if going faster would make the feelings go away faster, too. This wasn't the first time I was leaving what I wanted behind.

If I didn't leave him, he'd end up dead. History proved that to me over and over again. The moment I cared for someone, they got hurt. It was a curse.

Maybe it was because I was a demigod, but that didn't make anything better.

The road was mostly quiet, which only gave me time to stew. I sped through the countryside, wondering how long it would take to get to the next town. I'd been in Moirai for half a year and didn't realize how sparse it was once you leave the city this way.

Eventually, I would hit some sort of civilization.

I focused on the road and scowled, noting a figure standing in the distance. I wasn't seeing things, right?

"What the fuck?" I breathed.

I slowed as I came closer, and no, I wasn't seeing things.

Standing in the middle of the road was a man wearing a long coat like a long-lost vagabond. He was older, with gray hair and a face stamped in rage, I could see his pressed lips from here.

My heart immediately started racing. Something about him felt familiar, but I didn't recognize him.

I didn't know him and didn't plan to stop to get to know him. I'd seen these types of things on shows before. Someone pretended to need help on the side of the road, and then bam—

they kidnap you. I wouldn't fall for that sort of trap, so I sped up as I came closer, aiming to go around him.

The hairs on the back of my neck stood up. My eyes widened as I felt the atmosphere shift, realizing that I should have turned around instead.

It was too late.

The man raised his hand and I could smell the salt and brine of the ocean as my bike flipped and I sailed through the air, slamming against the road and rolling.

I came to a stop, but forced myself to keep moving. Whatever he was, he wasn't human—and my history in the last day and a half proved that most monsters sucked.

I got to my feet right as the man's boot came down where my head would have been.

"What the fuck is your problem?" I snarled, spinning out of the way as he lunged for me.

He moved faster than me. His fist collided with my gut and I gasped as I was sent sprawling back. I smacked the ground again, my head spinning.

Rage boiled hot and heavy as I got up again. I was really tired of being attacked like this. I wanted one goddamned day without someone trying to kill me. Why couldn't I be left to stew in my emotions?

The man lunged for me again, but this time, I met him with the same force. His stormy eyes flashed right before I punched him, hitting him square on the face. His head whipped back and he stumbled, clutching his nose.

"Who are you?" I growled again. "Why are you fighting me?"

He wiped the blood dripping from his nostrils and smiled an eerie, creepy, twisted kind of smile that made me feel deeply uncomfortable. "You smell like the Minoan Bull, Grim. Didn't someone tell you that it's a betrayal to fuck a monster?

You should know better. Then again, you know nothing right now."

"No, sorry, I missed the no monster fucking memo."

He sneered. "Pity. It is unfortunate things didn't go the way they were supposed to that night in the club. You've been on the run ever since. I wondered how deeply your mind has changed everything, but it's clear the methods worked. You don't even know me."

The club? What was he talking about? "I don't know what you mean," I said. "And I don't give a fuck."

"You wouldn't," he chuckled. "I made sure of that. You have failed and now you have to die. Since nothing else seems to have worked to kill you so far, it'll be at my hand. I can't let you live any longer."

I didn't like the way he said any of that. I held my hands up, wishing that he would let me go. "Listen, man. I'm leaving Moirai. I don't want anything to do with monsters or demigods or whatever business this is. I don't know you, you don't know me. Let me leave."

"You can't leave," he laughed.

"Why not?" Maybe getting him talking would work in my favor. The two of us slowly circled as we spoke, reminding me of a western stand-off.

"My name is Theseus, son of Poseidon, and the very last thing I'm going to allow into this fucking mafia is the Minoan Bull and his demigod fated mate. I should have killed you years ago."

My brows shot up because half of what he'd said sounded insane.

"He took the one I loved long ago. And the least I can do is make sure he never gets to have you. He doesn't deserve happiness."

I'd found plenty of dead bodies before, but I'd never killed someone. Hell, I'd never thought about killing someone until now.

The look in Theseus' eyes told me he would kill me.

He waved his hand and drew a fucking pitchfork from midair. The metal was deep cerulean blue, the air crackling with tension. It cast an eerie glow on his entire body, the wind picking up as if answering the call of the weapon.

"Well, that's fucking cool," I muttered.

Theseus gave me a cruel smile. "Sorry, you must die. Once, we would have been brothers in battle. But times have changed."

He rushed towards me again, moving in a dizzying blue. The two of us fell into a dance of him stabbing, me dodging, and wondering how in the hell I was supposed to go hand to hand with a pitch-fork wielding psycho.

I didn't have time to think. When he moved this time, it was like he'd leveled up, much to my despair. Fuck! I twirled out of the way just before he could skewer me, only for him to grab my jacket collar and yank me back.

We hit the ground again, and he brought the weapon down. The blades pierced me and I gasped, the pain excruciating as they went all the way through, digging into the asphalt.

The moment between life and death was my least favorite.

"I hate it has to be this way, but it does," he growled.

Once again, I was going to die. My eyes shut, the clouding darkness consuming me, taking control of me, ensnaring my soul.

But this time it was different.

"Twice in a row? Really?"

That annoying, grating voice was back. I opened my eyes, but I wasn't on the road, and I wasn't pinned beneath a demigod. I was standing in a dark cave in front of a shadowed figure that wore gray robes.

"Where am I?" I asked. "And who are you?"

"Charon," he answered. "Your personal guide, so it seems. Hades gave me one mission, and that was to deliver you to your mate and keep you from dying, and yet here you are, in the Underworld again. Your spirit must be tired."

I scowled. "Mate? Theseus said that too."

"Blech, I hate that guy. He tried to fight me once to see his girl. We kicked him out. When I get my hands on him one day, it'll be a wonderful time."

"Well, he killed me, I guess. And yes, by the way, my spirit is very tired. I don't understand why all of this is happening to me."

Charon shrugged, his shoulders moving. He cocked his head to the side. "You demigods are all the same, wondering about your fate and why things happen. You can't even remember who you are and you're worried about your fate. Not even I can answer that. The Fates are mysterious."

I shook my head. Even with the revelation of being a demigod, I didn't like the implication that my fate was controlled. "Well, I'm dead. So it doesn't matter."

"Not exactly. He's killed you for the moment, but you can't really die. Your daddy is too powerful for that. And diluted blood or not, you're still his son."

"Who is he?" I asked.

Charon snorted. I suppose this was what he really looked like, but it was strange as he didn't have a face with a perceivable expression. It was like staring into a pit of darkness, and the darkness laughing back. It should have creeped me out, but I found this easier than a talking bird.

"I'll give you three guesses. Use your brain, Grim."

I scowled, but I already had my guesses. I might not have been well versed in Greek mythology, but between Charon, the underworld, and not being able to die—

"Hades," I said.

I'd never felt something more true. The moment I said his name, I could feel strength surging through my muscles and veins.

Charon nodded. "Well done. I have to send you back now. The Fates surely have more plans for you."

Before I could ask more questions, he waved his hand, and the image of him rippled. I blinked, and I was looking back up at Theseus again, his spit dripping on my face as he snarled like a dog.

I grabbed the handle of the pitchfork...*trident* and his eyes widened as I shoved him back, ripping the weapon free of my body. It hurt so much I couldn't breathe, but then the pain quickly disappeared, soothed by whatever renewed strength I had.

I got to my feet and used the trident as a crutch, staring at Theseus. He reached for the weapon again and I shook my head.

"One more step and I break this in half."

"Give it back," he snarled.

He wouldn't give up. He grabbed me, and I let my instincts take over. It was quick and nasty, but I shoved the three sharp prongs into his chest, his rattled breath making me feel guilty as I twisted. Golden blood burst from his lips, his eyes widening.

"Well, well. That simply won't do."

A new voice. Great.

I looked over my shoulder. I'd been too engrossed in the fight to notice the sleek black car that had stopped in the middle of the road. The sun burned bright above us, casting another man's shadow over the asphalt. He wore a very expensive suit and had blonde hair and unnaturally bright green eyes.

"I don't know what you want, but I'm not buying," I growled as I twisted the trident.

Theseus rasped, the sound of his gargles making me feel sick.

The door to the car opened and yet another stepped out. He had dark hair, dark green eyes, and a menacing presence.

"This is what we get for leaving this to a demigod," the dark-haired one said. "He can't even stop his own pawn from slaughtering him."

"Yes, well. We're here now. And demigod or not, I don't think he'll escape us." The blonde one smiled. "Don't kill him. We'll capture him for now. The terms of our agreement can change, thank fuck."

Fuck my life.

"Are you demigods too? Is everyone in this fucking place a demigod?" I snarled.

He snorted, his smile thinning. "You're in luck. We're not demigods."

"We're monsters."

Chapter 8

The Labyrinth

Ryan

It had been a few hours since Grim left, and the absence of his presence left me feeling lonely.

Most of my men had returned to the house. They'd given me updates about yesterday—the car was totaled, my driver was dead, but the other guard survived. But he'd also quit, which was understandable since I'd left him on the side of the road. I would have quit if I were him. Jeff promised he wouldn't be an issue, at least.

Maybe I wasn't cut out to be a mafia boss. It wasn't because I was too soft, at least. I was capable of violence, of doing whatever was needed to keep people in line. That was the whole reason the Chimera twins used me in the past.

Killing, gutting, maiming, inflicting pain that could last

centuries. That's what I'd been made for. To kill demigods, you had to be strong and fierce and unyielding.

And here I was pining for one.

I shoved the thought away again, even though I knew it would come back to him. Grim was relentless.

I'd wanted to be in the Three Fates Mafia for so long, but now that I had it, I realized it didn't make me happy. It was a bitter pill to swallow after trying so hard to make it to this point.

If getting a free pass as a human, money, luxurious shelter, and anything I wanted didn't make me happy—what would?

Grim made me happy.

My heart felt like there was a lead weight sitting on top of it. It was absurd, but he returned to my thoughts like a fucking frisbee. It didn't matter how many times I tossed him away, he came back.

I leaned back in my desk chair, drumming my fingertips on the desk.

My body felt all the more restraining, like a lion forced back into a cage. I looked like a man, but I wasn't. Maybe that's why I was struggling. I was playing pretend in a house of knives, but I couldn't see the knives, and was supposed to pretend their sharp edges didn't hurt.

No wonder Percy and Madeline left.

My entire life, I'd dreamed about being another. Having a different face, having a different body, not being a monster, but being a man. The first century of my life, I'd been trapped in a labyrinth. And then I'd fought Theseus...

I'd been different back then. More monstrous, more bloodthirsty, ready to hurt and kill others with no care.

What happened to me?

Mostly, all I'd done today was stare at the wall, listen to updates, and try to justify why I shouldn't care about him. It had been a great night. A wonderful one-night stand, or second night stand if you consider the first time we were together. But that was it.

He was a demigod. I was a monster. Demigods and monsters did not mix, even if it worked out for a few others...

How could he ever want me to begin with? He only knew a little about me, and it was the brighter parts. He didn't know how many I'd killed, the things I'd done, the position I was in. I lead a fucking mafia branch, for fuck's sake.

Grim's life had been hard enough already.

He didn't need me in it.

Sending him away was an act of kindness, even if I wanted to keep him close. I'd let him leave, hoping that would keep him far away from my world. There was already too much happening, and I didn't want to risk him being mixed up in the mafia. The best thing he could do was get as far away from this place as he could.

I leaned back in my chair, staring at the ceiling. My office had a reflective tile ceiling, and I hated seeing myself. These eyes weren't my eyes, this face wasn't my face.

Ringing echoed through the room, and I sighed. I didn't want to talk to anyone, but I picked up my phone. I read Damon's name and answered.

"Yeah?"

"You never called me yesterday," Damon said, sounding irritated.

"I was busy yesterday," I said. "What happened on the phone?"

"Theseus did something idiotic and almost started a war. I don't trust him. I don't trust Orpheus either. Ever since Perseus and Madeline left, they've been working closer together."

True. But that seemed natural. "Why are you calling?"

He scoffed. "What do you mean, why? You said you found a fucking demigod."

"I did."

"And?"

"And he left this morning. Going off to some other city. We'll never see him again."

Damon's silence felt like the quiet between lightning and thunder. "Ryan, I have done a lot for you in the last few months. I've gotten to know you better, have helped you step into this mafia and learn. But this is the stupidest thing you've ever fucking done."

"He's not meant to be one of us."

"How do you know?"

I felt a streak of rage bubbling up. "Because I said so."

He growled. "How do you even know someone hasn't taken him? Did he leave your home? Did you put a tracking device on him?"

"Why would anyone do that? Why would I do that?"

"BECAUSE YOU HAVE ENEMIES NOW!" Damon roared. "Enemies that are looking for a weakness! Have you learned nothing?! You should have seen the state of the meeting room yesterday morning. You are in a delicate position and I am concerned they are conspiring against you."

"Who could be after me?" I snarled. "We have treaties in place."

"Those treaties only work to an extent, and they certainly don't apply to a new demigod, you idiot. Do you care about that demigod?"

"No," I lied.

"Be honest with me."

"I said no," I lied again.

"Then don't be surprised if he ends up dead on your doorstep."

Damon ended the call. I cursed under my breath and stood up, grabbing the edge of my desk and lifting. I flipped it, sending it tumbling over the floor.

The thought that anyone might try to hurt Grim set me on edge. I rolled my shoulders back, smoke drifting through the room. No one had seen us. I'd been careful about our transportation, right? Careful about making sure no one but Damon knew about him. And Damon wouldn't have betrayed me.

I grabbed my phone and called one of my men. He answered quickly.

"Find the man that was in my apartment yesterday. He was here at the house with me, too. I need to know if he's still on his way out of the city or not."

"Sir, do you have his number? It would be easier to track him."

Fuck me. I hadn't even grabbed his phone number.

Idiot.

"I don't."

"We will do our best."

"His name is Grim. He worked at a place where there was a murder yesterday. Said his boss was decapitated, and he's wanted by the police."

"That should help us get a number. I'll call you with updates."

I was about to hang up, but paused. "What's your name?"

"Elliot, sir."

"Elliot. Try to make this fast, okay?"

"I will."

I hung up, making a mental note to remember his name.

I needed to go after Grim.

A nervous knock at the door made my head snap up. One of my men winced, holding up a stack of envelopes. "You have mail..." His gaze drifted to the rest of the office, which was covered with the items previously on my desk.

"Leave them here. Get the fastest car I own ready."

"Yes, sir."

I had to find him. I'd start outside the city. Highway 181 would have been the logical way for him to leave, even if it went into a bit of farmland first before hitting other towns and cities.

I rushed out of the office and went to the front of the house, storming past blank faces. I'd been handed a mafia, and what had I done except step into shoes that didn't even fit?

Frustration continued to build as I stepped outside. A McLaren 750S waited for me in the driveway. I rushed down the steps and traded places with the driver, sliding into the front seat.

"Sir?"

I looked at him out the window. "I'm going after him. Everyone's instructions are to notify me as soon as he's been tracked."

He gave a curt nod, and I put the car in drive and slammed on the gas. The tires screeched as I took off.

I let my instincts take over, hoping they would lead me in the right direction. I peeled onto the highway and pressed the pedal, speeding as fast as I could. The trees zipped by and I kept the windows rolled down, inhaling the air like my life depended on it.

Maybe mine didn't, but maybe his did.

You better be okay.

My chest tightened the longer I drove. A glint of metal caught my eye on the side of the road and I cursed under my breath as I pulled off to the side. I desperately looked for blood or a body as I shoved the door open. The bike was mine, but Grim was nowhere to be found.

Damon's words came back to haunt me.

I had enemies. I already knew that, but seeing the wrecked bike and no sign of Grim meant they were closer than I'd expected. It was foolish to think they weren't watching my every move.

To think that they wouldn't have wondered about Grim.

The highway was empty. I stepped onto the road, looking for any other signs of struggle. A flash of gold caught my attention, and I knelt down.

Demigod blood, but not his.

I swiped my finger over it and brought it to my nose, inhaling the scent.

It was familiar. In fact, it was one I could never forget.

Theseus.

"You son of a bitch," I whispered.

My phone went off in my pocket. I straightened and pulled it out.

Unknown: Call off your search. Come to The Labyrinth. We have your demigod. Come alone, or else.

Fury made my hands tremble as I texted back.

Me: I am going to slaughter you.

It took every ounce of control not to crush my phone. I stalked back to the car and slid in, slamming the door shut. My eyes shut and I reminded myself to breathe. To think. Whoever had taken Grim thought they were using him to overpower me. They were trying to use him to manipulate me, but why?

Theseus clearly still hated me. His blood on the asphalt meant he was involved. Had he acted alone or was there someone else involved? My thoughts swirled as I turned the car around and merged back onto the highway, heading straight for Moirai. It would take at least an hour to get there, but that also meant the sun would set.

Darkness would be my friend, especially in a club like The Labyrinth.

Who the fuck had named that place, anyway?

I scowled as I drove faster.

I went through every scenario I could think of as I drove. Theseus didn't have the largest branch of the mafia, but his men were trained and loyal. Not to mention, where Theseus was, Orpheus typically was too these days.

As for the other factions…I couldn't count the Chimera twins out. And I couldn't count the Hydras out either. While the Hydras had shown no animosity to me yet, they were still cold and calculating. If I had anything they wanted, now would be the time to make their move.

I twisted in my seat and leaned back, feeling for a latch on the floorboard. I kept my eyes on the road until I felt it and twisted, opening the hatch. I glanced back quickly, seeing that my weapon stash was fully stocked.

I made sure that every vehicle I had was stocked like this. It made me feel like a super villain, but it was necessary given I was in a mafia.

I hit the Moirai City limits with a plan for murder. It wasn't long before I pulled down the street and into a valet spot outside the club. I looked up, seeing the flashing red sign that burned The Labyrinth into the dusk. A stone of dread settled in my gut as I leaned back and grabbed the weapons I wanted, stowing them away on my body.

I got out and passed my keys to the valet, along with cash from my wallet. I didn't even look at him as I took in the club. There was a line outside of people waiting. The bouncer at the door was a big guy, tougher than before.

Was I just going to go in the normal way?

I'd never run a rescue mission before.

My phone beeped in my pocket. I stepped onto the sidewalk as I pulled it out.

Unknown: Meet us at the red door inside.

I pressed my lips together. The nerves I felt were a combination of concern for Grim and concern that this situation ran deeper than I could glean.

Despite their warning to come alone, they said nothing about me telling someone else about the situation. I shot Damon a quick text message and then tucked my phone in my pocket, walking straight for the bouncer guarding the door.

He gave me a curt nod and stepped aside, allowing me in with ease.

The club was how I remembered it. The music was heavy, the scent of sex making my mouth water. Lights flashed, highlighting the bodies that pressed against each other.

I thought about Grim, silently praying he was okay. He was a demigod, so he should have been, but...

I'd killed plenty of demigods in my lifetime.

If someone got ahold of him that knew how...

My stomach twisted as I pushed through the gyrating bodies. The deeper into the club I went, the more erotic the sights. If and when all of this chaos ended, I wanted to come back here with Grim. Put on a public display, showing the world that he was mine.

The possessiveness that hit me was fierce and unyielding. My mouth watered as I shoved that primal desire into the back of my mind.

His safety was my priority. That and fucking up whomever had taken him in the first place. If it was Theseus, then I would make him regret everything.

My gaze swept over the mortals, zeroing in on the dark hall.

I didn't like where this was taking me. My skin crawled as I wove through the crowd. The hallway was absent of anyone as I came to the beginning of it.

The red door was at the end. I glanced over my shoulder, making sure no one was looking. I reached into my jacket and clutched my gun, withdrawing it as I crept forward slowly. I listened for anything out of the ordinary, breathing in the scents.

I didn't smell Theseus.

I frowned as I came to the end of the hall. The red door loomed in front of me.

Was Grim behind it? I could feel my phone rattling in my pocket, but I ignored it. I reached for the doorknob and twisted, pushing open the door.

The room was not the same. In fact, it didn't even appear to be a modern building, but a dark cave.

Every instinct told me to run.

"I can't do this," I whispered.

I'd find another way to get Grim.

I spun around, but firm hands grabbed me and shoved me forward with a force that was beyond mortal. I hit my knees hard, landing on cold stone.

"Sorry, Ryan. It had to be this way. We can't have you in this mafia."

I turned around, horror filling me. Paris, one of the Chimera twins, stood in the doorway, which now hovered above me.

I let out a roar and lunged to my feet. "What are you doing?"

"Putting you back where you belong. I don't want this, I should add. But a deal has been made, and you were just collateral."

His voice was so cold, his expression like stone.

"Don't do this," I rasped. "Please, Paris."

Something flickered in his gaze, but he shook his head. "I'm sorry, Ryan."

I reached for him, but he slammed the door before I could grab him, and it blinked out of existence.

No.

No, no, no.

"Very funny!" I called, unable to keep the desperation from my voice. It became difficult to breathe, ice flooding my veins. "What is this, Paris?! We had an agreement!"

My voice echoed off the walls.

Fuck.

The silence was heavy and all too familiar.

I reached into my pocket quickly to pull out my phone, but the signal was completely dead.

Of course technology wouldn't work here.

Panic rose up like a tidal wave and I fell to my knees, my heart thundering in my chest. I closed my eyes, my head ringing as I tried to control the emotions, but they warred against each other with such a ferocity that I couldn't breathe.

They always put me back in this place.

Why did they always put me back in this place?

For centuries, I was forced into the Labyrinth. That was even how Hercules fucked me over the last time. The darkness, the endless mazes that lead nowhere and everywhere, but there was no escaping unless someone opened a door from the outside. I felt everything closing in again. I'd had it all and yet again it was robbed from me because I wasn't good enough.

Because they didn't see me as their equal.

I roared loud enough that my human form split, and I let it. I tore it away, wanting to be as far from the lie as I possibly could. I screamed as I changed, my body searing with pain as it released, and I became who I really was.

The demigods hated me.

The monsters didn't accept me.

What did they want me to be? What did I have to do? They feared I would ruin their lives, and...

If I ever made my way out of here again, I would.

I would make their fears come true. Their own self-fulfilled prophecies in the making, and I would see them through.

The worst part of this was that I still didn't know if Grim was okay.

Chapter 9

Grim the Unfriendly Ghost

Grim

Hot, fiery pain radiated through my body, and unfortunately not the fun kind. I groaned as I forced my eyes open, blinking through the impending darkness. I wasn't sure where I was, but it sure as hell wasn't anywhere good.

I tried to move and found that I was confined by chains. I strained against them, but it was no use. I was sitting up in an uncomfortable metal chair. The only bit of light in the room was a green prick, which meant that there was a camera in here. Aside from that, I could see nothing else.

My nostrils flared, and I breathed in deep. There was no notable scent, and nothing familiar.

I tugged against the chains again, rage balling up inside me. I remembered what happened now. I'd fought that old bastard on the road and the only reason he won was because two monsters interfered.

That fight had sucked. In fact, both fights had sucked. Even though my body healed from the wounds Theseus gave me, it still ached.

And then whatever fucking monster the other two bastards formed?

They'd put me through the wringer. Their tail's spiked end had nearly severed my neck, which was apparently enough to make me pass out for some time.

All I wanted at this point was a whisky and coke and a monster-demigod free life.

"If you let me go, I'll leave for good," I called, glowering at the solid green light. "I don't even want to be here. You can let me leave and I'll never come back again."

No answer.

Of course not.

If I couldn't die, then the possibility of being left to suffer forever became very real, and that didn't sound great at all. I moved my fingers behind my back, wincing as numbness prickled into feeling. It was uncomfortable, but better than letting myself not feel.

Why was this happening? I replayed what I could remember that Theseus said. None of it made any sense to me. I'd never met him before, right?

The way he'd spoken to me...

I lost track of time. My body continued to ache, and I continued to fight to keep my limbs awake.

Occasionally, I pulled against the chains, or even let my head fall forward to sleep. I wasn't sure what else I was supposed to do. It didn't matter how hard I tried, the chains certainly would not budge. And yelling at the camera that I could barely see helped nothing either.

Eventually, my thoughts turned back to Ryan. I thought about everything that happened in the last day, from the decapitated boss, to sleeping with a monster, to fighting a monster and losing.

It was a series of unfortunate events that didn't fit together quite yet.

For the last six months, I'd been changing jobs frequently and living out of hotels. Always keeping a low profile. Why? When I tried to think about that too much, my head pounded. Frustration rolled through me.

What was happening to me? Why?

The pitchfork psycho mentioned the phrase 'fated mate'.

Out of everything he said, that was what stuck out the most at the moment. I wasn't sure what a fated mate was, but if it was anything like the animal kingdom, I did know what a mate was. It sounded barbaric, and strange, but if what he said was true then maybe I was supposed to be with Ryan...

The fact that I was kidnapped and now chained up in a room, but thinking about my second night stand really said something about my priorities.

Being with him had been a few hours of pure bliss. I'd never been fucked like that. If I could live in his room of BDSM equipment then I would forever.

I should have been long gone by now.

If my hands weren't chained behind my back, I would've flipped off the camera. Irritation rolled through me the longer I thought about things.

I didn't ask to be a demigod, if that was even a real thing. And I certainly didn't ask to be mixed up in all of this madness.

Where was the talking bird when I needed him?

I glowered into the darkness, wishing that I could be free. My stomach grumbled with hunger, reminding me I hadn't eaten today. And gods knew what time it was. Eventually I would have to take a piss and I really didn't want to do that in this chair. I also really wanted to have another go with those slimy bastards.

If supposedly my father was a god, and specifically Hades, then why couldn't I break these chains? Shouldn't I be strong enough to get out? What was the point of having an all-powerful parent if you couldn't escape a dangerous situation?

My mother died when I was very young. I remembered little about her, but the more time I had to think, I recalled her telling me stories. Stories about the Underworld, about the gods, and how death wasn't scary. Perfect topics for a toddler.

Hades was the god of death. Perhaps that's why my entire life had been plagued by it.

The past six months were especially difficult. But maybe something happened the night I slept with Ryan at the club. I could remember the sex perfectly well, but everything else about that night felt like a hazy dream.

He was a monster, after all, and ingrained in this underworld of myths and reality. Maybe that experience brought my unusual condition as a demigod to the forefront of everything.

He probably thought I was long gone by now.

In fact, he'd probably already forgotten about me.

I tipped my head back, staring at the ceiling. At least, I thought there was a ceiling. I blinked a few times, trying to make out any sort of shapes.

It felt like there was nothing.

Aside from the green light, I felt like I was trapped inside of one of those sensory deprivation tanks. The silence itself was deafening.

My heart pounded faster, the idea of being stuck here forever sending a wave of panic through me. I did my best to keep it at bay, but it curled through me.

I've been through this before.

That thought struck me from nowhere, and I did my best to ignore it. I couldn't remember a time I was locked up like this.

The shittiest part was that no one would miss me. I let that settle in and it sobered me enough that my heart stopped beating so loud, replaced by a sense of sadness.

No one would miss me. No one would look for me. I would just be another number for the statistics.

Everyone that I ever loved died. Just like I told Ryan, it was dangerous to care about me. So, on the bright side, for once at least I was the one that was in trouble.

Time lost meaning again. Exhaustion washed over me, my eyes closing slowly as I gave into sleep.

As soon as I dozed off, I was standing outside of my body.

What the fuck?

I could see myself in the darkness, chained to the chair. I looked down at my other self, seeing a pale, ghostly outline.

Either I'd died again or I'd just discovered a perk of being the son of Hades.

Ghostwalking.

I tried taking a step back and found that I could move freely. I laughed and did a little dance, flipping off the camera with both hands.

What else could I do?

I stepped behind the chair I was tied in and my brows shot up. No wonder I couldn't move. The chains were reinforced with rods across the back, and they were heavier than any I'd seen before. I knelt down and reached for the padlock.

The moment I touched it, a burning sensation started, as if my effort to stay this way had increased tenfold. I could hold the lock though, just as I could if I weren't...Grim the Ghost.

Muffled voices drew my attention. I raised my head and looked to the left. I drifted closer to the wall and pressed my hands against it, surprised that they pushed through.

I had no idea how this worked, but I was going to roll with it for now.

I frowned and pushed myself through, stepping out on the other side of the wall. It was a dingy hallway with swaying jaundiced lights. Two men stood at the end, arguing.

I recognized the two bastards. They were monsters.

The dark-haired one was furious. He leaned against the wall, crossing his arms. "I don't agree with this. I don't. We never work with the elder demigods. It's never worked out. And since when do we turn our backs on our own?"

"We need what he offers. That is why we are doing this," the blonde one argued. "You know this."

He shook his head. "It's not worth it. To capture a new blood? I agreed with that. To throw the Minoan Bull back into the Labyrinth? That is not what I agreed to. The things that Theseus has done without the rest of us knowing...we should bring this to the others. This is cruel."

"We are cruel. This world is cruel. And the price Theseus put on his head was too great to resist. Let go of your morals, help me finish this fucking job, and then let us reap the rewards. Did you do it or not?"

The dark-haired one lingered for a moment and then shook his head, still clearly enraged. "Yes, I fucking did it. You're on your own for the rest of this, though."

He disappeared behind a heavy door, leaving the blonde one alone.

He slumped against the wall when he was alone, blowing out a heavy breath. I found it interesting how different he appeared at this moment. His shoulders relaxed, his brows drawing together.

That guy was a bastard, but I still felt a bit sorry for him. Only a little, though.

Finally, he looked up, glancing down the hall. I froze, wondering if he could see me.

I watched him slide on his invisible armor again. He straightened and rolled his neck, his eyes lighting up with anger and hatred. He stalked down the hall and came to a door.

Fuck, he was going into my prison room.

I stepped back through the wall, shivering. It felt weird to pass through something. Nausea shot through me as I rushed to my body. I knelt down behind the chair and grabbed the lock, yanking it as hard as I could. To my pleasant surprise, the metal snapped, the chains loosening. I reached out instinctively. The moment I touched my shoulder, my eyes opened again.

I was whole again.

The scent of metal filled my nostrils, blood dripping down my face.

Fuck.

Unexpected consequence.

The chains were loose though. And he was coming in alone.

Together, I couldn't fight the two of them yet, but alone…

The door cracked open, light flooding the darkness. I blinked, my eyes burning as he stepped in.

"You've got shit luck," he sighed. He stepped close to me and grabbed my chin, forcing me to look up. His nostrils flared at the sight of blood. "What's this, huh? Demigod blood?"

He leaned in, his tongue snaking out and swiping up a drop. I pulled back, looking at him like he was insane.

He hummed. "Well, you're not my mate. That much is true."

"Oh course I'm not," I snarled. "What the fuck is wrong with you?"

"Surprisingly, not a lot. I have the task of taking you somewhere special. Are you going to cooperate or are you going to fight?"

"What do you think?" I asked pleasantly.

His eyes flickered with unnatural light. There was a heavy silence, and I decided it was now or never.

All of my pent up anger and frustration from the last two days bulldozed its way to the surface as I gripped the chains around me and jumped up, unraveling them like whips. He stepped back, the surprise offering a moment of advantage.

I kicked at his knee hard enough that bone crunched. He let out a monstrous roar as he went down and I wrapped the chain around his neck, pulling with enough strength that he went still.

"Is this your plan?" he growled. "To try to kill me? I don't die easily."

"If I pull your head off your neck, I think it'd be pretty tough to keep living."

He chuckled, which honestly pissed me off. I grabbed his head and twisted, the neck bones snapping and his body going limp. He fell forward, hitting his head on the edge of the metal chair.

"Oof, buddy," I winced.

He wasn't getting back up yet. I wavered on my feet and forced myself to breathe, wiping my face of blood from the nosebleed. I squatted down and felt his body for any weapons, pulling out a knife and a gun.

It would have to do.

I felt his phone too and tossed it to the concrete floor. I smashed the screen with the heel of my boot and then rushed out of the room, sprinting down the hall. I made it to the door and opened it slowly, peeking to see what was behind it.

A rough hand grabbed me from behind.

Fuck.

"When you see your fucking mate, have him tell you how to really kill a monster, you miserable bastard."

He shoved me forward through the door and I fell into a cold, dark cavern. When I looked up, there was nothing there.

It was like I'd fallen into a completely different world.

"What the fuck?" I snarled.

I looked around again, bewildered. The darkness wasn't infinite, which meant there had to be a light source somewhere. I could make out the rocky walls and cavern ceiling, which had jutted stalactite teeth hanging down.

A roar rumbled in the distance, coming from the dark mouth about twenty feet in front of me.

I frowned. Logically, hearing a beastly roar should have driven me in the opposite direction, but I'd heard it before. I forced myself to breathe and got to my feet, glancing up again. The door was gone for good, it seemed.

I wasn't at a point where I was going to try to understand how that happened yet, but eventually would get answers. Fingers crossed.

The roar echoed through the caverns again. I crept towards the tunnel, sending a silent prayer to the gods, fates, or whatever ran my luck that my instincts were right.

"Ryan?" I yelled.

The roaring stopped.

"Ryan?!" I shouted again. "Is that you?!"

I swallowed hard as I waited. The sound of hooves on rock came first, followed by a menacing figure galloping from the darkness. I barely had a moment to process until he barreled into me, pinning me to the cold floor beneath his Minotaur form.

"Are you real?" he rasped.

"Yes," I whispered.

"How do I know?"

There was actual fear in his voice. Smoke puffed from his nostrils, his eyes burning like embers. His muscles rippled, his hurried pants concerning me.

I reached up slowly and pressed my palm against his cheek. "I'm real," I whispered.

He sucked in a breath. He was silent for a moment before he murmured. "I've damned us both. I'm so sorry, Grim. I didn't think they would throw you in here."

"I think I probably damned you," I snorted. "Considering my history."

He leaned down and kissed me, a monstrously strange kiss that made me melt beneath him. He held me there for a moment, drinking me in like I was his savior, even though I felt like I'd doomed us both.

He released me and rolled to the side, landing on his back next to me.

"What is this place?" I whispered.

"The Labyrinth."

"Not the club...."

"No. Unfortunately not. Although that is how I ended up here again. Where were you, Grim? It was the twins that took you."

"Twins?"

"They don't look like twins, but—"

"Oh, those bastards." I glowered. "Yeah. It was them and Theseus, who I fought and defeated, but then they showed up and..."

"You fought Theseus?" Ryan asked, turning over onto his side.

I felt like I was retelling battles and history, but in a weird pillow talk caveman way. He tugged me closer, his warmth a comfort.

"I fought him. He's an asshole. He made it very clear he

didn't want you to have me. They keep calling me your mate. Is that what I think it is?"

He grumbled and cleared his throat. "Maybe?" he wheezed.

I narrowed my eyes. "Care to explain?"

He sighed dramatically. "I have a lot of things to talk about, and this wasn't exactly what I expected to be first..."

"What is a fated mate?"

Chapter 10

Switch

Ryan

Grim waited for me to answer, and it was clear he wasn't letting it go. The problem was, I'd been fighting this thought for the last 24 hours, and now I had to give the question some sort of answer.

Fated mates.

It was the dream for a monster like me.

Someone meant for you that loved you. Cared for you. Saw past the dark parts of your soul, or even embraced them. They were the candle in the never-ending night, a glowing warm soul to hold onto when the storms raged on.

For centuries, I had pined for the dream.

And now, I had Grim. And I couldn't deny that I wanted him to be the one.

"Fuck," I snarled, drawing in a sharp breath. I didn't know how to explain everything.

I was still reeling from the fact that he was even here with me.

The twins had worked with Theseus to trap me, which was a twist I hadn't foreseen. They hated Theseus, which meant he had something they wanted. Whatever that was, it had to be worth them betraying a monster like them—which was also concerning.

I despised feeling like a fool. If and when we got out of here, I was going to destroy all of them. I would make them pay for ever crossing me like this, especially Theseus.

The rage dug its heels in, twisting through me as I held onto it.

"Ryan? It's not a bad thing, is it?"

"No," I whispered. "It's not a bad thing at all."

I focused on him, studying his face in the dark. There was a bit of golden blood on his face and I licked my thumb, reaching up to wipe it away, even if a lick of it would tell me if he was meant to be mine.

I wouldn't test that until he wanted to. Every instinct told me to do it now, to find out if we were bound together, but as much of a brute as I was—I didn't want to force him into anything. Fate or not.

"Fated mates are exactly what they sound like. Your soul mate. The one meant to be yours. Your destiny. Your one and only."

He let out a low snicker. "You sound very bitter."

"I am," I mumbled. "It happens to some monsters, but..."

"Can't happen to you?"

I was silent. Yes, that's what I'd believed. It didn't matter that I knew of other monsters who had found the one that loved them, that they loved too. It didn't matter that logically I understood there could be some out there for me.

"Why can't it happen to you?" he asked softly.

I struggled to speak, but Grim pushed me over onto my back and shocked me by straddling me, running his hands up my chest. He leaned in and kissed me gently before sitting back.

"We make our own choices," he said. "I'm new to this world. Brand fucking new. And I realize there are things I don't understand, but I can say for sure as a gay man in his thirties that has seen people live, die, love, and hate—you choose who you love, Ryan. The idea that there is someone out there who is perfect for you is a myth. Love takes work."

I knew it took work. Even fated mates didn't have perfect lives. But...

"It's more than the idea that someone is perfect for you. It's that your imperfections complement each other," I said. "It's your blood, it's a connection that humans don't understand. And you're not a human, but you've lived as one until now. I can't explain it until...unless..." I trailed off, unable to finish my sentence. "You do choose who you love. To have a fated mate—it's like an offering from the gods, a promise of a connection that will complete you. That doesn't mean you have to."

He thought about that. I could see his thoughts spinning as he digested the implication. "So they think we belong together."

"Apparently," I said hoarsely, unable to stop the way that idea made me feel. Fucking hell, I wanted it so badly. I wanted him so badly it hurt. "Which is why you're now stuck in the Labyrinth with me...I'm sorry."

"Don't be sorry. At least we're not alone," he said. "And, well...if I had to be stuck with anyone, I'm glad that it's you."

My cock started to harden, and my nostrils flared. I closed

my eyes, trying to keep the lust at bay. It seemed impossible when he was with me. "Are we certain your parent isn't Aphrodite?" I muttered.

He chuckled. "It's Hades, actually. I learned when I died again, ended up in the Underworld, and talked to a ghostly blob named Charon. Oh, and apparently I can turn into a ghost? I'm learning a lot about myself and I'm not sure any of it will help our unfortunate situation. How do we get out of here?"

"We don't," I sighed. "I'm sorry. This entire situation shouldn't have happened to begin with. I should have realized they would target you."

He pressed his lips together. "Well. No one will miss me."

"I would have missed you," I mumbled.

His face softened, and he leaned forward and kissed me, running his hands up my chest. And fuck it, this time, I didn't contain what I wanted. I let out a low growl and gripped his hips, sliding him down so he could feel my cock pressing against him.

His eyes widened. "Now?" he huffed.

"I was ready to take out an entire branch of our mafia for you tonight."

"Fuck. That's hot. Murder shouldn't turn me on."

"Well, you are Hades' son."

He made a noise and moved his hips, grinding against my cock. I stared up at him in wonder, thankful that while I was in another terrible situation, he was here with me. That I wasn't alone this time.

My cock pulsed against him, desire rolling through me. Every time I saw him or was around him, I wanted him so fiercely that it frightened me.

"I have a suggestion," he rasped.

"I'm listening..."

"I think we should perhaps take some of our frustrations out on each other and then we can talk and devise a plan."

I didn't have the heart to remind him there wasn't much to make a plan, but I still nodded. "Agreed."

His eyes sparked with excitement and he leaned down, circling one of my nipples with the teasing tip of his tongue.

"Oh fuck," I whimpered.

He kept teasing me, circling and sucking. All of my worries and anger and sadness melted beneath his touch. He took it slowly, teasing one and then the other. I moaned as he went back and forth, my cock straining against him.

We had a million problems to think about, but I couldn't think of a single one of them the longer he touched me. I melted beneath him, drinking in his presence, feeling like I never had before.

I reached up and slid my hand around his throat, grabbing him firmly. His breath hitched, his eyes raising to mine. I let out a low growl and flipped him over, rolling him beneath me. He shivered, his cheeks flushing as I kept my grip on him firm.

"I could fuck you for hours," I snarled. "Every moment with you, I can't think straight. All I can think about is pumping my cock inside of you over and over."

He wet his bottom lips, his breathing rough. "And?"

I narrowed my gaze, his sassy attitude going straight to my cock. "And let's see how long we can go before you beg me to stop, little king."

"You're underestimating my appetite for monster cock," he whispered.

I squeezed harder, and he grunted, his eyes fluttering as I controlled his breath. I reached between us with my free hand and gripped his cock, feeling how erect he was. I listened to the sounds he made, a series of involuntary moans that I was causing.

That brought me pleasure.

Fuck. We might have been stuck in the Labyrinth, but we could make use of our time.

I stroked him faster, watching his expression closely. I huffed in his scent, my mouth watering as my instincts begged for a taste of his blood.

"Fuck," he moaned, his hips thrusting up.

I kept stroking him until he was about to come and then released his cock.

His eyes flew open, the defiance making me chuckle. He glowered at me. "I was so close," he complained.

"And?"

Turning that word back on him now brought me immense pleasure, especially with the way he struggled against me. I released his throat and grabbed his arms, planning to pin his wrists above his head, but he shoved me hard—surprising me with his demigod strength.

He let out a growl, pushing against my chest. I fought to get hold of his wrists, grabbing them only to lose my grips as he tore them free. My cock throbbed as we wrestled, my size overwhelming him, even though his strength was shocking.

"If you're going to fight me, demigod, then fight me," I snarled.

We struggled against each other until I managed to roll him onto his stomach, mounting his hips and holding both of his wrists down against the cavern floor.

He moved one arm up and the other down in a quick motion, throwing off my balance. I fell forward as he locked his legs with mine and rolled me over onto my back.

"Gotcha," he growled, grabbing my cock.

The moment both of his hands closed around my shaft, I let out a guttural groan, my hips bucking involuntarily.

"You bastard," I groaned.

He smirked victoriously as he ran them up and down. "Are you going to behave now?"

I narrowed my gaze at him. The give and take dynamic we were falling into was exciting. "Yes," I whispered.

"Yes, *Sir*."

There was silence between us for a moment, and then I very softly said, "Yes, Sir."

I wanted to please him. That realization hit me so hard that I sucked in a breath right as he leaned down, fitting the head of my cock in his mouth. He held my gaze as he sucked, working his tongue artfully.

"Fuck you," I sighed.

I closed my eyes, pleasure winding through me as he kept sucking. The sounds he made were almost enough to make me come. I moaned as he worked me faster. His palms were rough and felt good.

He pulled his mouth free and grabbed my thighs, motioning for me to pull them back. I hesitated for a moment, but then did as he asked, pulling my legs back and exposing myself completely to him.

Grim cupped my balls, rolling their heavy weights gently. "Do you want me to fuck you, little bull?"

Little bull.

Fuck.

Fuck.

I could barely think straight as he waited for my answer. He cocked his head. "Too much?"

"No," I said roughly. "No...you just keep shocking me."

"I think it's a fitting pet name," he murmured. "If you like it."

"I do." My throat felt tight as he smiled.

He leaned down and kissed the head of my cock gently, still playing with my balls. He dropped a glob of saliva onto his palm and used it to work my hole gently, probing me with two fingers. I whimpered and closed my eyes.

"I appreciate your trust," he whispered. "And I appreciate that you'll let me touch you like this, especially knowing that you're dominant too…"

All I could do was nod. He kept working me and slipped a third finger in, readying me for his cock. Pleasure seared me, hot and fiery but sweet and calming. I wanted him to fuck me and fill me, and then I wanted to flip him over and do the same thing.

"Grim," I growled. "I need you to fuck me now."

"I will," he huffed. "Not yet."

"Please."

"Oh?" He cocked his head as he looked at me, his lips tugging into a smile. "You sound good when you say please, little bull."

I shuddered, but I said it again. "Please. *Please.*"

He braced his hands on the backs of my thighs and pushed, leaning into them as he lined his cock up with my hole. I moaned as he pushed forward, driving inside of me. I fixed my gaze on him as he took me, reveling in his expressions of bliss and lust.

The man that I'd bound, gagged, spanked, and bred was the same man that could turn me into a begging puddle. That duality turned me on in a way I hadn't expected. Knowing that he wanted me both ways…

Mate.

He was my mate. I knew that as he drove his cock completely inside of me, his groan music to my ears. I knew that as he looked at me, the light in his eyes burning through my darkness. I drank him in as he pumped into me, his cock thrusting in and out.

"Fuck," I huffed, losing myself to the feeling of being taken.

He grabbed my cock and stroked as he drove in and out, his hips a rapid piston. I fought the urge to come, but the control was hanging by a thread.

"You feel so fucking good," he moaned. "I don't care if we're here forever. Fuck."

The harder he fucked me, the more I realized I didn't care if we were stuck here forever, either.

Chapter 11

Breeding Milk

G^{rim}

My cock was deep inside Ryan, his monster balls bouncing as I fucked him. I stroked his massive shaft as I buried myself inside of him over and over, pleasure lighting through me like a live wire.

I could do this every day, I realized.

When I was with him, I lost track of time. I lost track of reality. I grunted as I looked down at his Minotaur body, drinking in every muscle and curve. His nose ring glinted gold, just like the one at the head of his cock.

"Harder," he gasped.

His wish was my command. I drove into him with even more power, leaning into his body as I took him. I knew that more than likely the moment I was done, he'd flip me over and have his way with me—but that was part of the excitement.

Knowing that I could make him whimper when he could make me beg.

It was what I'd always wanted. To be with someone who could be dominant or submissive, and that could handle both sides of me as well. Because as much as I loved giving, I enjoyed taking too.

Especially when taking from someone as hot as him.

I slammed into him fully, grunting as I fought the need to come. I wanted to drag this out as long as I could.

Ryan growled loud enough that it echoed through the caverns, a deep rumbling. I panted, sweat slicking my body as I worked him. He clenched me harder as he milked my cock.

"I'm so close," I huffed. "Fuck."

"Come inside me," he moaned. "Please."

Every time he said please, my breath hitched.

I was railing a Minotaur, and that was almost hotter than anything else I'd ever done.

"Please, Sir."

Fuck me. I couldn't hold back now. Not with him calling me *Sir* like that. I threw my head back as I fucked him harder until I let out a guttural growl, my hot come bursting from me and filling him.

I moaned as I came, pumping it all inside. There was so much of it, and even then, there was more. He stayed still as I came inside of him, his breaths coming out in harsh smoky puffs.

I collapsed forward, out of breath again. He slid his arms around me, holding me tight as I came down from the high of the orgasm.

He chuckled and ran his fingers through my hair. "You came so much," he whispered, sounding impressed. It certainly wasn't as much as he could, but for a human...

I nodded, breathing in his musky scent. It was becoming all too comforting the longer I knew him.

I should have been panicking about being stuck in a goddamn supernatural cave, but couldn't find a shred of worry. I felt like I was floating on the clouds, wrapped in a shroud of ethereal peace.

He growled in my ear, his grip on me tighter than before. "My turn."

I squeaked as he pulled me out of him and then turned me over onto my back. I spread out beneath him, my eyes widening as he leaned down and dragged his tongue down my chest. He paused to suck my nipples, and those small motions made me thirst for more.

"Ryan," I whispered.

He chuckled and drew back. His broad hands clasped me and he once again showed his brute strength by turning me clockwise until my face was right beneath his massive cock and balls.

Precum beaded at the head and dripped, landing on the tip of my tongue.

The taste of him was like a drug. I closed my eyes as all the nerve endings in my body came to life, my head spinning. I looked up at his bobbing cock and reached for it, stroking it lovingly and guiding the head down.

I prodded the slit with my tongue, and he shuddered. More cum splashed into my mouth and I swallowed it down, the pleasure increasing more.

"Your cum is like a fucking aphrodisiac," I huffed.

"For my mate, it is," he grunted.

My eyes widened as I licked my lips. There was that word again. Mate.

"Do you want to mate me?" I whispered.

"*Grim*," he snarled as his cock grew thicker. "Don't play

games with me. Shut up and suck my cock like a good boy."

Well then.

He angled his hips and pressed the head of his cock to my mouth, thrusting forward. I moaned as he shoved between my lips, the bulbous head cramming against the back of my throat. My eyes rolled back as he withdrew and drove forward again, the feeling of being throat fucked mercilessly turning me on.

"You're such a good slut," he snarled. "The perfect fuck hole for me. Do you like being used?"

All I could do was nod, but only for a moment before he slammed into me again. I yelped as the head pushed in deeper and I couldn't breathe, my airways literally cock-blocked.

"Fuck, you're so tight," he huffed. "I can feel your throat pulsing around me. Mine."

Heat spread through me like a wildfire. I forced myself to breathe through my nose as more of his addictive seed spilled down my throat. I felt his hot breath on my body and then he pulled my legs back, the tip of his tongue rimming me.

I couldn't scream, because his cock was still deep down my throat, but I sure tried. Pleasure rippled through me as he drove his hot tongue into me, holding me in place as he plunged his thick cock in and out, using me how he pleased.

His movements were rough and demanding and sent me tumbling into a headspace that was akin to flying. I moaned around his cock as his tongue moved in and out of me, my cock hardening helplessly.

He pulled back suddenly, and I sputtered, choking in breaths as he released me. He turned me over roughly and dragged me around so that I was on all fours beneath him, his cock nestled between my thighs.

"Beg me for my cock," he whispered. "Beg me to breed your little hole."

Fuck.

I was panting as I spoke, my words breathless. "Please breed me. Please. I need you inside of me."

His monstrous form sent a shiver of need up my spine. I moaned as he shoved me forward, spreading my ass and using his spit to lube me up. The head of his cock pressed against me as his broad hand landed on my upper back, shoving my chest against the floor, ass up in the air.

"Oh gods," I whimpered as he pressed against me.

He held my hips in place. Heat poured off his body in waves, rolling over me as he pushed forward. I cried out as he gave me the first part of his cock, but I knew there was more to come.

My fingers dug into the dirt, and I pressed my ass back as I met his thrust. He groaned as he took me, pumping into me again and again. He worked more of his cock inside of me, pushing it in further until I was taking every single inch. The sound of his balls slapping against me resounded through the cavern.

"You feel so fucking good, demigod," he huffed.

I panted as I twisted, looking back over my shoulder at him. I liked it when he was rough and I liked it even more when he said demigod like that.

He met my gaze, his eyes burning hearths in the dimness.

"I'm going to breed you every hour and every fucking day we're in here," he huffed. "Until the end of time."

My eyes fluttered as he slammed into me, impaling me with his hot shaft. Pleasure built faster and faster, and while I'd already come, I knew he would make me burst again.

"Damn you," I groaned.

Ryan chuckled victoriously before driving in harder and faster. My eyes damn near rolled back as I took him. The sound of his pants grew faster, his touch more demanding as he got closer to the edge.

"Breed me," I begged. "Breed me."

It became a chant as he drove into me. I whimpered and moaned and begged as I took him, everything else falling away. He grunted as he thrust harder, his fingers digging into me.

I wanted him to leave marks on me.

I wanted him to mark me as his.

"Fuck, I'm going to come," he rasped.

With one more firm pump, the two of us groaned together as he came. Heat splashed inside of me as every muscle relaxed. He let out a soft groan and pulled out, his cum dripping down my inner thigh.

"We're a mess," I rasped.

"Perhaps we can find a hot spring," he chuckled.

"Are there some here in the Labyrinth?"

"Occasionally the path guides you there...There were times when I was alone that I found things I needed. This place is strange."

I nodded and gave him an appreciative look. "Tell me about it," I said softly.

He scowled. "Tell you about what?"

"Your time here. Your life."

When he looked at me, I could sense that he was holding back. I was patient, though, and certainly not going anywhere.

"Come on," I murmured. "I know you're a monster. I know that you're in the Three Fates Mafia."

"Yes," he grunted, spreading out next to me.

I rolled over onto my back, splaying out. There was a gap of space between us, and while we'd now fucked countless times, my heart hammered as I closed the space by slipping my hand into his.

"If I tell you about my life, you won't want to know me."

"Who on earth ever made you think that?" I asked.

He tensed and started to pull away, but my grip tightened.

"You can't run," I teased. "The worst you can do right now is tell me no, which I'd respect if you chose to."

Ryan shook his massive head and then sighed, finally relaxing next to me. "I'm not good, Grim. Monsters are feared and hated for a reason…I've killed people. I've hurt them. Tortured them. Even recently, I hurt people who didn't deserve it." He shivered, but his hand only tightened around mine, as if he were now holding onto the only person who'd probably really listened to him. "You shouldn't even be with me. I should have made sure you got far away from Moirai. I should have—"

"They would have found me, eventually. They were determined. We can't control what they did to us," I said. "In all the things I've seen from humanity, that's the biggest thing I'd say monsters, demigods, gods even…all have in common with us. When they decide to do something, they do it without thinking about how it might hurt others. Because those others don't matter."

He drew in a sharp breath. "True."

The silence settled between us, and I expected that he wouldn't share. My eyes started to close, but then he finally spoke.

"I was made to kill demigods. My father was a monster sent to a queen as a joke by the gods. I was birthed and locked away, a royal secret that eventually became a weapon. I don't really know how long I was here for the first time. Time moves differently between here and there, and it sometimes changes. More than likely, if we escaped now, it will have been a couple of weeks on the outside. Or it could be two hundred years."

"Fuck," I whispered.

"Mortals would sometimes wander in, wanting a claim to fame. Kill or maim the Minotaur. Seek fortune. But then they'd die. Either I killed them or the Labyrinth consumed them. Then came Theseus."

"I hate him," I muttered, thinking of the crazy bastard who'd challenged me on the road. I rubbed my chest, thinking about the trident he'd pinned me down with.

"When he was a young man, he was different. He was probably good. I was bad. I'm not going to mince words, Grim. I was a monster. Every year, they sacrificed men and women to me. He was sent in to kill me and end the sacrifices. His beloved gave him a string to lead him back out of the Labyrinth."

I frowned. "I think I've heard this story at some point."

"Well, they said that he killed me and left the Labyrinth. They also said that she sailed with him, was left on an island, and that Theseus forgot to change the color of his sails as promised to his father—who then killed himself."

"Fuck. That sucks. But you're not dead..."

"No," he whispered. "She followed him in and got lost. He and I fought violently enough that we were both severely injured. She came upon us and attacked me."

His silence told me what he didn't want to say. I swallowed hard, still squeezing his hand.

"How can you lie here with me?" he whispered.

There was so much pain in his voice.

"How can you stand me?"

"It was a long time ago, and she attacked you."

"I ripped her heart out of her chest and threw it at Theseus' feet."

Well, fuck. I wasn't sure what to say to that. "So...Theseus lied about killing you?"

"I begged him to say that he did so I could be left in peace. He vowed vengeance, but ultimately left. In his grief, he forgot to change the sails, which led to his father's death. Every demigod has a tragic story. Every hero ends up carrying the weight of a world that wants to bleed them dry on their shoulders. And every monster is a tool made by the gods to stab them over and over and over. And it doesn't matter what you want. It doesn't matter if you don't want them to wield you."

"But the demigods are their children," I whispered.

"And they were the children of Titans once, whom they cut into pieces and buried in Tartarus. Look at your life, Grim. You've seen death over and over when you shouldn't have."

"Yeah," I sighed. "I have."

"That was just my beginning. Apply that tragedy to centuries of pain and suffering and being manipulated."

I snorted, which was definitely not the appropriate reaction. He gave me a quizzical glance. "Sorry," I whispered. "I'm not laughing at you. I just...you're rather balanced for someone who has been through so much."

"Grim, I am not fucking balanced."

We looked at each other and stared until I burst out laughing. He stared at me like I'd lost my mind, but I couldn't help it.

"I'm not either," I said, wiping my eyes. "We probably need therapy."

Ryan blurted out a laugh. "I'm not sure a therapist would be helpful."

"You'd be surprised. Really, the Three Fates Mafia should have one on standby. Here, let me talk to you about that myth that happened centuries ago and how it affected your self-worth."

I winced, realizing how sharp my words were, but Ryan rolled his eyes.

"Fuck you," he said.

"You just did."

He chuckled again and leaned over, kissing my forehead. I smiled, the silly warmth spreading through my chest again.

"I think the Fates made us for each other. I'm not sure what that means for the rest of the world, though," I whispered.

He mumbled under his breath and then brought my knuckles to his lips, kissing them. "What it means for now is that you should rest. I'm going to find what I can to build a fire so you don't freeze to death."

"I can't actually die, according to the guardian of the underworld."

"I'm still going to build a fire. Sleep, little king."

I nodded and curled into myself. He grabbed my shirt and draped it over me. Despite being on a rock floor and trapped in a place that shouldn't even exist, I fell asleep quickly.

Chapter 12

Flames

Ryan

I LEFT Grim for a few minutes to see if I could gather things to burn or create a fire. To my luck, I found rocks, wood, and with a little digging—enough of it to build a fire.

By the time I made my way back to him, Grim was fast asleep. His snore was painfully cute, his chest rising and falling with each breath.

I couldn't help but smile like an idiot.

I couldn't help but wonder if that's how it would be if we slept together. Him having a little snore while I creeped on him, romantically of course.

I spent the next hour or so building a fire. It had been a long time since I had to build a fire, but I managed to get sparks flying and wood burning. It kindled slowly at first and then built up, burning bright and casting a warm glow over the cave around us.

Finding such items was a stroke of luck. I sank down to the floor and listened to the wood crackle, the scent of wood smoke comforting. Humans didn't depend on fires to survive anymore. Living in the city, it was strange at times to see how much their world had changed.

And how the Fates had adapted us monsters within it.

The flames grew higher as I stared into the fire, thinking about the past and how I'd changed and clawed my way into this world.

When I'd been trapped here the first time, it hadn't been uncommon for mortals to stumble in. If we saw skulls in the corners or buried in the dirt, it was more than likely put there by my hands. And if not...

The Labyrinth, now so timeworn, was a graveyard for lost souls.

Some of them died here. Some of them, by chance, escaped.

My sense of direction lost all meaning in this winding darkness, and in a terrifying way, that was a comfort. It was the place the poets and storytellers said I belonged, a place where a monster like me was meant to be bound.

I'd told Grim there was no way out, but only because I didn't want to give him false hope. I still wanted us to escape. There had to be a way to do so, even if all the times I'd left had simply been luck or fate or whatever you wanted to call it.

I wanted to get him out.

It wasn't fair for him to be trapped here with me. He'd done nothing to deserve this. I'd underestimated the envy and ferocity of Theseus. Everything that Damon said over our call about expecting Grim dead on my doorstep could have become a reality.

In a way, we'd been lucky with how things had gone, especially since he didn't act alone.

I couldn't understand why Theseus would attack another demigod so fiercely. I wasn't sure his hate for me was enough. And I also wasn't entirely sure how he'd concluded that Grim was my mate and meant something to me.

Grim was being hunted when he fell on my car.

I pressed my lips together, thinking about things. There were parts of this puzzle that didn't make sense.

The monsters I'd seen on the overpass...they were not natural beasts. They were man made, or...

Demigod made.

I wished I had more answers, but perhaps time would give them to us.

Time moved differently between the Labyrinth and the outside world. Here, we could be trapped for a day or two, and it would be weeks in the regular world or longer. Or shorter. I couldn't decipher the whims of the maze. It was a blessing, but it also could be a curse.

The first hundred years I was in this place had passed quickly and bloodily. From the infamous King Minos sending sacrifices into the maze to the demigods that attacked me...All of it felt as clear as a myth.

When I'd come out on the other side of that time period, it was another world.

One that I'd struggled to understand.

The mortal's empires rose and fell in the blink of an eye. Every few centuries, one would come into power, only to snuff itself out. I'd long ago stopped paying attention to their politics, and only recently started trying to learn again since I was indeed a part of their world.

I didn't want Grim to miss out on the world he was born into.

I didn't want that for us.

For us.

I rubbed my chest absentmindedly as I thought about what would happen if we escaped. We'd need to get to Cerberus or the Colchian Dragon before the others found us.

Rage simmered the longer I thought about it, and I went through a handful of fake scenarios that all ended with me beheading our fucking enemies and running off into the sunset with Grim like some romance novel.

Fighting my imaginary scenes wouldn't help us, even if it made me feel slightly better.

Grim let out a soft snore and curled into himself more. I turned my attention to him and scooted closer, hoping my warmth and the fire would keep him from being too cold.

He was a demigod, but that mortal part of him was so fragile, it frightened me. Every hour that went by was an hour I felt closer to him, and my worry that I would fail him again sank its claws in deeper.

In a world where any sort of vulnerability was to be exploited, certainly falling in love was the greatest weakness of all. And yet, I could feel it taking root and growing, and nothing I said to myself could stop the feeling from blooming.

It scared the fuck out of me.

The urge to mate him—truly mate him—was so strong that even the thought made my cock perk back up. I breathed in deep, but the air was intertwined with his scent.

"Fuck," I mumbled.

I hungered for him. Every waking moment, he was on my mind. And I imagined that if I did sleep, he would be in my dreams too.

Grim let out a soft hum and sleepily lifted his head, his sleepy gaze fixating on me.

"Go back to sleep," I said gently. "You're safe. I was being loud, my apologies."

He nodded and sighed contentedly, eyes shuttering closed and body relaxing again.

My heart felt like a bucket of confused emotions and a resistance to them that was being worn down. I wanted him so much that it hurt. But I didn't deserve him.

I couldn't make up for everything I'd done.

I wasn't like Damon. I wasn't even like Ian or some of the other monsters that could look at their sins and move on. I saw the blood on my hands and worried I would hurt Grim. I was a mafia boss, a monster, and a terrible person, but in thinking about spending a life with him—I wanted to be more than those things.

I wanted to be more than what the world said I was.

For him.

I breathed out.

What would our future even look like? If I let myself love him, if I gave myself that chance...

Would the Fates want him?

Would he become like the other new demigods?

I couldn't see him enjoying leading a mafia. He'd already seen so much death. But he was the son of Hades. Perhaps murder was an acquired taste, after all.

My thoughts went in a circle while Grim slept. It was an endless spiral that didn't end until the fire turned to embers, the wood burning out.

"Fuck," I muttered.

I got up and went to the pile I'd gathered, cursing myself as I brought pieces back to the flames, working to rekindle them.

Once Grim woke up, we would need to make a plan.

Some sort of plan.

As much as I enjoyed the thought of being here forever

with him, he had a life to live. And in theory, I still had a mafia branch to lead.

I had the sudden vision of Grim leading it with me, which was something I hadn't truly considered. I closed my eyes, reveling in the thought of having that life with him.

Waking up and going to Moonie's.

Working and then playing.

Living in the house with him. Or the apartment. He could decorate it however he wanted. When I'd bought the big house, I had an interior designer create all the spaces, and while they were masculine and warm—I knew he would make them better.

He would make it feel like home.

Breaking in all my unused BDSM equipment would be an adventure. There were so many things the two of us could do together. I imagined myself on my knees for him while he teased me, tortured me...

I smiled to myself and opened my eyes. The fire was burning brighter now.

Maybe that could work. Maybe, just maybe, the two of us could find some happiness in the world.

Maybe I could stop being a useless tool to the gods.

I breathed out and sat back, my muscles finally relaxing. I glanced over at Grim again, watching his brows pull together in his sleep. The firelight danced, catching his beards and the dark hairs that furled on his chest.

The artists would have worshiped him.

The poets would have pined for him.

The bards would have sung about him.

And here I was, a monster, wondering if I could love him. And it wasn't if I *could* love him, I'd already fallen for him—it was did I even have the right to.

No one had ever looked at me the way he did. No one ever wanted me. No one ever saw past the walls I'd built until now.

And it unnerved me.

Scared me.

Made me wonder what the Fates really wanted from me. Why had they chosen me? There were other monsters in this world that were probably far more deserving.

"Why me?" I whispered earnestly. I doubted the Fates even listened, but I still spoke as if they were. "Why us? I don't deserve him. How could I ever earn his love?"

I shook my head and hands, as if shaking would let my emotions free.

"I love him. And I have no fucking clue what to do about it except pray to the gods that hate us to please keep him safe. I will do anything to keep him safe."

Chapter 13

The Underworld

rim

I was a ghost again.

I cursed to myself as I hovered over my body and Ryan. He wasn't sleeping, his gaze fixated on the flames of the fire he'd built. He looked tense. He rolled his shoulders and neck, his hands shaking.

I lingered for a moment, worried that something had happened.

"Please keep him safe," he whispered.

Did he mean me?

He glanced over at my sleeping body.

Yeah.

Yeah, he meant me.

Damn it, I was really falling for the guy.

I looked down at my body again and wondered what had

happened. One moment I was dreaming, then the next I was out of my body. I turned around and looked down the cave, feeling an inexplicable pull.

I didn't like that.

My ghostly body seemed to lead the way. I stole one more look at myself and Ryan and then allowed myself to drift through the cavern, making my way down the winding path. I couldn't feel the chill in the air, and the darkness didn't keep me from seeing perfectly.

Perks of being a ghoul? Or son of Hades? I wasn't sure.

If I were in any real danger, Charon would interfere... wouldn't he? I contemplated that for a bit because to be honest, he seemed morally ambiguous at best, and I wasn't sure he would actually help me if it came down to it.

When I glanced back again, I realized I'd come a lot further than I thought. I could no longer see the fire Ryan built. It was nothing but the darkness and a winding passage that seemed to stretch on.

What happened if I couldn't find my body again?

Fear curled through me, but I decided potentially being unattached to my body forever was a problem for later me.

I rolled my shoulders back and continued down the passage, allowing whatever feeling this was to tug me along. In my ghostly form, my heart didn't hammer in my chest, but mentally it sure as hell did. I slowed as the passage narrowed.

A door.

My eyes widened. Nestled in the rock was the faint outline of an ancient-looking door made of stone. The symbols chiseled into it looked old, which was about as far as my knowledge of such things went.

"You aren't meant to open that door."

The voice startled me. I spun around, surprised to see a man standing there with dark slicked back hair, onyx eyes, and tan skin. He wore a suit, but that didn't disguise the waves of ethereal power rolling off of him.

I knew who he was.

And I was thankful that in my ghost form, I wore clothes instead of being ass naked like I was in my body back at the fire.

"Hades," I whispered.

The corner of his mouth tugged into a smile. "Yes. That door leads to the Underworld, but the form you are in now would get lost. It would be difficult to return you to your body."

"Oh..." I trailed off and took a few steps away from the door, easing closer to him. "Do you happen to have a handbook on how to be a demigod?"

"If I did, your uncle would steal it and burn it."

"Wonderful," I muttered.

Hades chuckled. "I can't stay long, and I am not supposed to interfere with this world. But you're in the Labyrinth, and most gods cannot perceive this place well. It is fair ground to meet you on."

I nodded, my throat closing up. I had a lot of things I'd always imagined saying to my father if I ever met him, but all of them went up in smoke. I couldn't think of a damn thing.

His eyes softened, and he stepped closer, clapping his hand on my shoulder. "The life of our children is difficult. I know yours has been hard. I know that death comes for you, but it is a gift. Death itself is not evil. Death can be a beautiful thing. You'll see that in time."

"I don't understand why things are happening," I sighed.

"The Fates have their mysteries. You are a demigod in a world that no longer believes in us. You're young and powerful, but you don't understand those powers yet. And your mind has been tampered with by another. I am here to lift those walls so that you can see things clearer, and then I must go."

"Tampered with?" I echoed.

Sadness filled his gaze. "I'm sorry. This might hurt you. Know that when you speak to me, I listen. And if I can help you, I always will."

He reached up and touched my temples. There was a shock of power, but that wasn't what hurt.

It was the flood of memories that did.

"What are you doing?" I cried out.

My foster parent shoved me through the doors of a warehouse. The scent of blood filled the air, terrorizing me.

"I found one," his gruff voice said, shoving me forward.

I was only sixteen, but already in my brief life, I'd seen too much death. The man that stood behind me was my foster father. He despised me. I could feel the hatred coming off of him and I feared for my life.

It wasn't supposed to be like this. They were supposed to love me. To care for me. But I knew that would never happen. None of the adults that took me in ever loved me for long.

The man in front of me was one I'd never seen before. He had bright blue eyes and silver hair. He studied me like I was an insect, a feeling that made me feel sick.

"How do you know?"

"Everyone dies around him. My wife..."

I winced, trying to shove the feelings away. It wasn't my fault. It wasn't my fault that she died. I didn't do anything.

"I didn't kill her," I rasped.

"You shut up!" he bellowed, hitting me hard at the back of my head.

Pain burst, my mind swimming as I fought to stay upright.

"That's not enough proof," the man said, shrugging. "People die all the time."

"He can't die either. I tried."

He buried a blade in my back and I cried out, my knees buckling. The pain enveloped me, everything turning black for a few moments. This wasn't the first time he'd done this to me. The night his wife died, he'd stabbed me over and over and over and—

When I opened my eyes, I was right back in reality, on my knees between the two of them.

Now, the blue-eyed man was interested.

"I see," he whispered. He leaned down, his face hovering in front of mine. "How old are you?"

"Sixteen," I rasped. "Please let me go."

"I'll give you a better life."

"I just want to be free," I said. "Please."

He studied me and then nodded. "I'll give you all the freedom you can imagine. Aren't you tired of them hurting you?"

He waited for my answer.

The truth was yes.

I was tired.

I was so fucking tired.

"Yes," I whispered.

"And this man hurt you."

I nodded, numbness settling over me like a cold weight.

He raised his hand. "Leave."

"Well, I want my money—"

I gasped as he moved in a lethal blur. Blood splashed over me, hot and sticky. I looked up, realizing that he'd shoved his hand through my foster parent's chest, taking his heart out.

Terror filled me as the body collapsed to the floor.

He looked down at me, his expression softening, but I could still see the cruelty in his gaze. "My name is Theseus. And you, my friend, are in for a new life. One where the mortals can't hurt you anymore."

I gasped, doubling over and retching. Theseus. I'd known Theseus for years. For years.

More memories rushed through my mind, stabbing me with their sharp, shiny blades.

"Kill him."

The voice of Theseus pushed me on. I stared down at the mortal before me, feeling their life in my hands. I was their reaper, and it felt good to be that.

"Please don't," the mortal whispered. "Please."

Just a mortal. Just a regular mortal. They didn't mean anything. They didn't matter like we did.

I looked up at Theseus. His arms were behind his back like an expectant father, waiting for me to do as he commanded.

Just do it.

Make him happy.

Just kill him.

I twisted the mortal's head, cracking his neck with ease. The sounds sent a shiver up my spine. When he died, I could see his soul hovering briefly before disappearing.

"Good. Very good. Again."

"No," I sobbed. "What the fuck? Why?" Why had I done those things? I was a weapon for him, a tool he was sharpening with hate.

To hate the monsters.

To fight and kill them one day.

To hate the mortals too.

The memories wouldn't stop.

"Did he make you kill again, Grim?"

I looked up at Valerie as she came into the library. I was seated on a bench next to a massive arched window, the moon shedding light on the gardens below. I couldn't remember the last time I'd slept.

She wore all black, dried blood speckling her warm brown skin as she neared me. I could see the death clinging to her, a cloak she didn't want to wear, but did.

Just like I did.

She stepped closer to me and knelt down, cupping my face.

"You can't lose faith," she whispered. "One day, we'll escape him. One day, he won't control us. I've been hearing things. Visions of the future. Of what's in store."

I shook my head, fearing for her. "Be careful, Valerie. We're just tools to him. You can't say these things aloud. He might hear us."

The punishment for saying such things was brutal. We were demigods, and dying was not so easy, especially for me. He'd kept me in a dark cell with no sound or light for days once. Goosebumps erupted over my skin at the thought of going back to that place.

"But we are as strong as him," she insisted softly. "We're just younger and still understanding our powers. He can't keep us caged for so long. We have our own destinies."

Destiny. I shook my head. I couldn't see a destiny for any of us that ended in something good.

A scream echoed through the halls. I winced, feeling the pain all the way to my bones.

"He caught another one," I whispered. "A woman. She's a little older than us."

"He did. But he's trading her to three monsters."

"I thought he hated the monsters?!"

"He does. But he's still using her to appease them. I think they discovered his secret."

I shook my head, disgust and hate rolling through me.

We were his greatest secrets.

"I've been trapped for years. An assassin for him, a secret weapon. He took me in when I was sixteen. I'll never escape him," I whispered. "I've killed so many for him. I've done awful things, Val. This is my destiny."

"Have faith," Valerie clucked. "He can't control us forever.

He should know that's how the Titans died. History repeats itself."

I breathed out, a sob shaking me. Valerie. She was still in danger. When was the last time I'd seen her?

Fuck.

"FUCK!" I shouted, rage bursting through me. "What the fuck is this?!"

Hades knelt down next to me. "Theseus has been grooming you for years. You've been a secret kept from the mafia, kept from the monsters and other demigods. He secretly hunts for others like you."

"Valerie," I rasped. "She's..."

"She's still trapped. But you escaped."

Everything that I'd been doing since that night in the club made sense now. Working jobs that were low profile, hiding, moving, running. It was instincts that were driving me. Driving me to hide from Theseus.

I shook my head, tears rolling down my face. I hated him. I hated him so much. Theseus had taken so much from me. From her.

No one had stopped him.

"I'm going to kill him," I whispered.

"He is not yours to kill, Grim."

I sat back. Not remembering anything had been a blessing, and Hades had taken that from me.

I wasn't who I thought I was.

I wasn't who Ryan thought I was.

"Ryan," I whispered. "Fuck. He's going to hate me. I was supposed to kill him."

"The night you were with the Minoan Bull, you were sent to slaughter him. But he is your fated mate. And there is power in that sort of connection, a power that disrupted Theseus' hold on you. You won't have suppressed memories anymore, Grim. And he can never manipulate you. Free Valerie from him."

Hades placed his hand on my shoulder and I sucked in a breath, my eyes closing.

"Remember that you are the son of Hades," he whispered. "Remember that you are stronger than him. And remember that you are not alone. And also...you can open a door in this place. It is close to the Underworld, and you can get out. You can save yourself and your mate."

With that, he left me alone in the dark, everything that I knew about myself and the world shattering like fragile glass.

Chapter 14

Confessions

R^yan

I shook Grim again, sweat dripping from me. His heart was still beating, he was still breathing, but he wouldn't wake up.

"Grim," I snarled. "Wake the fuck up!"

Tears rolled down his cheeks. Panic gripped me and I shook him harder.

"Please, please," I begged. "Wake up!"

His eyes flew open, and he gasped for air.

I dragged him into my arms, relief flooding me. "Thank the gods," I sighed. "What the fuck was that?"

He shoved me back fiercely enough that I fell on my butt. I was surprised as he got up, storming as he gathered his clothes quickly, putting them on.

"Grim?" I asked softly.

There was something different about him. His movements, the way he held himself, the haunted expression.

"Did you have a nightmare?"

"Don't speak to me right now," he whispered. "I need...I need a moment. Please."

The please was so desperate. My eyes widened as ran his fingers through his hair, pacing back and forth. A heavy feeling settled over me.

Maybe I'd done something wrong.

"I'm here for you—"

"Just shut up!" he shouted, his voice echoing through the cavern.

I immediately went silent. I could feel my own walls going up as I watched him. I'd done something wrong. Maybe he'd heard me talking earlier.

My throat burned. My chest felt like an elephant sat on it.

"I am not who you think I am," he hissed angrily. "I am not...fuck. FUCK!"

His shout rang again, and this time, I got to my hooves. Whatever was happening, I couldn't stand to see him like this. I reached for him, but he shoved back, his strength more than I'd ever felt before. I growled, grabbing hold of him and refusing to let go.

"Fuck off," he snarled, shoving against me. "I said fuck off!"

The two of us wrestled, and he didn't hold back. I grunted as he slammed me into the wall, his expression darkened with hate and...

Pain.

I knew that face.

I knew that look.

I grabbed him by the throat and shoved him hard, slamming him into the ground. His breath knocked out of him as I mounted him, pinning him beneath me.

"Grim," I breathed heavily. "Tell me what the fuck is happening."

He stared up at me, fighting at the hand around his throat, until his eyes widened. Tears glimmered until they fell, streaming down his cheeks as a sob shook his entire body.

"Grim," I said his name softly. "What is happening?"

"I saw my father. I saw Hades. I saw him and he...he freed my mind. I had memories that were being suppressed. Memories about who I really am."

I blew out a breath and loosened my grip, but he shook his head, holding my hand there.

"You'll hate me," he said, his voice trembling.

"Grim, I could never hate you."

"But you don't know me. You don't know—"

"Whatever you have done in your past can be no worse than what I've done. Look at me. Look at me." I forced him to meet my gaze and leaned down, my hand still clasping him. "Tell me. Let me in."

"Theseus took me when I was sixteen. He's been using me over the past fourteen years as a weapon, a secret tool to hurt others. He hates monsters. He hates mortals. He sought out demigods before others could find them so he could manipulate and train us. I'm not the only one."

"Fuck," I whispered, sitting back.

That motherfucker.

"I've killed so many people, Ryan. Innocent people. I've killed other monsters. I've killed...fuck."

His voice broke, and I slid off him, dragging him into my lap. I held him close to me as he shattered, my arms tightening around him.

"I've done so many bad things. I was supposed to kill you at the club that night, but something happened. Being with you changed me. I escaped and I've been running since, but I didn't realize it because of how he has our minds manipulated. There were gaps in what we could remember, and if we ever left him, we were supposed to become helpless. To forget who we were. I'm so sorry. You should hate me."

"I don't hate you," I rasped. "Fucking hell, Grim. I don't hate you at all. You were a child at sixteen."

He trembled as he spoke. "My foster parent brought me to him. He wanted money for me."

I let out another string of curses. I'd never felt anger like this. It pooled in my gut, a hot molten lava of rage and vengeance.

"He killed me in front of Theseus to prove I couldn't die. And then Theseus ripped out his heart and promised me the world. I believed him for the first few years, but...when he found Valerie, he did so much to her. And the other...he traded her to monsters."

"What monsters?" I growled.

"I don't know. I don't."

I drew in a deep breath, trying to steady my growing rage. "So, there are more," I whispered.

"Yes. I think that's how the Chimera became involved. I think they want Valerie."

I let out a low growl. "We are going to escape. And then we are going to expose him and save her."

His breath hitched, and he shook his head. "I can't. What if he kills you?"

I chuckled, holding him tighter. "He won't kill me. We have allies. More than half of the mafia despise him. And once they know he's been hurting demigods...We can do this."

"I'm so sorry," he whispered. "I'm so sorry I lied to you."

"You didn't lie. You didn't know. He manipulated you."

"I feel like a fraud."

I tipped his face up, wiping away the tears that dampened

his long lashes. "You look way too pretty when you cry," I murmured. "So let's save the tears for when I'm fucking you, okay?"

Now he laughed. I wiped the rest of them away and kissed his forehead, letting out a sigh.

"I'm sorry I yelled at you."

"It's okay," I murmured.

"Is it?"

He leaned up and grabbed hold of my face.

"I'm sorry. I shouldn't have yelled, but I was freaking out, and these memories are flooding back. I still feel guilty for what I was supposed to do," he whispered.

"Grim, I forgive you," I said.

He stared at me for a moment longer and then nodded, relaxing. He settled in my lap, his hands roaming over my chest.

"I have a confession," he whispered.

"Tell me, little sinner," I said, teasing him enough that he smiled.

I realized I would do anything to make him happy. The thought of sixteen-year-old Grim being hurt over and over and then sold off to Theseus infuriated me more than anything ever had before. I wanted to wreak havoc on everyone that had ever hurt him.

Grim snorted. "I can feel the violence coming off of you, my love."

"Can you?"

"Yes. Well...now that I'm remembering things, I was a lot more...attuned to my abilities. I know some of what I can do."

I nodded, interested in what that would mean. "And you're a son to Hades. I'm sure your power is extensive. In the old world, demigods like you didn't exist. He doesn't have children."

His eyes lit up with curiosity. "Really?"

"I've never met one until you. Theseus probably suspected when he realized you couldn't die. That's not an attribute that would belong to another god or goddess."

He nodded, mulling it over. "Hades told me Theseus is not mine to kill."

"Then he's mine," I muttered.

He shook his head. "No. I think there is more to this. But we won't know until we leave. Also, I never made my confession."

I cocked my head. "Confess, then."

"I'm falling in love with you. And there's a part of me that's like Fates be damned, while the other part of me knows that being with you feels right. When I'm with you, everything feels possible. I feel seen. I feel loved. And I just...I want this. With you."

I closed my eyes and pressed my forehead to his. "I don't deserve your love."

"You can't say that after everything you've just learned about me. You deserve my love."

I didn't argue, but I still couldn't believe it entirely. Still, what he said made me feel joy unlike anything before.

"I can get us out of here," Grim said softly. "I'm able to open a door out. This place is close to the Underworld, and supposedly means my power is stronger."

My eyes widened. "Do you know how?"

"I have...I have an idea. And I'm going to take us to a place where we can be safe."

"The penthouse would be best," I said. "If it's a possibility. And we can hope that it hasn't been too long."

"Hopefully. Up to the Fates, right?"

There was a bitterness to his voice, but I understood. I'd

struggled with the Fates for a lot longer, and it was difficult to trust they had anything good in mind.

Grim kissed my cheek and then rose. He pulled his shoulders back as I stood up, his nostrils flaring as he breathed out. He held out his hands to mine, and I took them.

Immediately, I could feel the power prickling at his fingertips. It was like a static shock, my fur raising up. He held my gaze, but he wasn't looking at me. It was like he was looking past me, to a plane I could not see.

"Close your eyes," he rasped.

His voice sent a chill down my spine. It didn't sound like him. I closed my eyes, holding onto his hands even as the static became stronger. A wind whipped up around us as a thousand voices wailed, a chorus of the dead singing around us.

Suddenly, it felt like we were falling.

My grip tightened so hard I worried I would crush his hands, but he held firm. I fought the urge to open my eyes, but I didn't want to see where we were.

The wailing grew louder, the wind harsher than blades as we tumbled through a portal.

I slammed against the unyielding floor and Grim landed on top of me. I groaned as he rolled off me, feeling a soft rug against my back.

"You can open your eyes," he panted.

I did and grinned. "You did it. You got us here."

The two of us were sprawled out in the living room of my penthouse apartment. The lights were off and it was quiet, the evening sky dark purple as it turned to night outside.

I rolled over onto my stomach, staring out at the city.

"You did it," I whispered again.

Grim let out a little moan and held up a shaky thumbs up. I leaned over and kissed him fiercely on the mouth, over and over until he started laughing.

"Okay, okay. Yes, I did it."

He chuckled as I kissed him again, and this time, he grabbed one of my horns and held me in place, his lips parting for me as our kiss became more sexual. He groaned against me, his hand cupping one of my pecs as he circled a nipple with his thumb.

I drew back, breathless. "Fuck," I rasped.

"We have enemies to defeat," he whispered.

"We do."

"But I think a hot shower and you fucking me would be a great precursor to crushing them."

"Agreed," I grunted. "I want to check the security system and locks first."

He nodded, and I got up, going to the front door and doing just that. Everything appeared to be secure. I then went to a series of switches and flipped one, which brought an automatic blackout curtain down in front of every window.

"Smart," he called. "So they don't know."

I nodded, my cock already hardening as I went back to him.

I picked him up and carried him bridal style through the apartment, taking him to the massive bathroom with a walk-in shower.

"We made it," I whispered softly.

Chapter 15

Mated by the Minotaur

Grim

I never thought a shower would feel so fucking good.

Hot water ran down my body as Ryan lathered up soap, rubbing my muscles and making me moan. We hadn't been gone long, but I still felt filthy, and between the two of us—we sent a lot of dirt and grime down the drain.

His hands were firm and comforting as he touched me.

Everything was coming back in waves. Another memory washed over me and I stiffened. But he was patient and soft. He rubbed me, whispered softly as I fought back a sob, every muscle in my body tensing as I relived terrible things.

"I'm not a good person," I said weakly.

Theseus had used me for so many awful things so he didn't get his hands dirty. I wondered if the rest of the mafia had any idea how much he did behind the scenes. The underground of Moirai was a bloody, fierce place.

"You are," he reminded me gently. "You are a good person."

"I killed a man simply for pissing me off once. I reaped his soul like it meant nothing, and then he haunted me for two years. And I realized the things Theseus made me do were wrong. Fuck."

"Breathe," he whispered. "Keep talking it out if it helps."

I blinked back tears. "I always had to hide if a monster was nearby because we weren't supposed to be detected. One time, I was almost found out, and Theseus locked me in a room with no light or sound or anything for days. I don't know how long really. I can't remember."

Ryan let out a low snarl. "That son of a bitch. I'm going to slaughter him…"

I squeezed my eyes shut, tears falling. Ryan reached around and wiped them away, his body relaxing again.

"I'm here for you," he said softly. "I'm here."

My breath was shaky. Everything from the last few years—hell, the last decade—was rolling through me. All the closed wounds were reopened stitch by bloody stitch.

"Breathe," Ryan whispered.

But I wasn't alone.

"I'm here, little king."

Ryan was here with me.

His soft words brought me back to reality.

"Touch me," I rasped. "Please. Make me forget."

"I can't make you forget," he whispered. "But I can certainly make you feel good."

"Please," I whimpered.

I needed him now more than ever.

I groaned and tipped my head back, resting it against his

broad chest. He reached around and circled my nipples, his cock hardening as he kept playing with me.

"Ryan," I rasped.

He nuzzled my neck. A shiver of need went through me as he growled. The low rumble reverberated through his entire body.

"I've waited so long for someone like you," he whispered. "And I don't know how, but you've ended up in my life and I want you to stay here forever."

"I want that too," I whispered.

"Get down on your knees and suck my cock."

"Yes, Sir," I said.

He let out a grumble of satisfaction. I knew how much it pleased him to be called *Sir*.

I turned around and sank to the floor in front of him, stroking his throbbing cock. He let out a soft groan, his head tipping back. The bathroom lights glinted against his golden horns, the ring through his nose gleaming.

I cupped his balls, massaging them gently between my hands. I leaned forward, dragging my tongue up his shaft, desperate to taste him.

"Fuck," Ryan grunted. "I need to take you to bed. But first, I want you to worship my cock."

I nodded eagerly. Pleasing him was keeping me from truly falling apart.

He let out another moan as I sucked one of his balls into my mouth, massaging them with my tongue. I gripped the base of his cock and then made my way back up, fitting the head between my lips. I tugged on the cock ring with my tongue, enjoying the sounds he made, egging me on.

His fingers dug into my hair and he pushed forward, filling my mouth and throat. I loved it when he choked me like this. He held my head in place as he forced his cock deeper.

I choked and coughed around him, but he kept me firmly in place. My eyes watered, my head spinning.

He thrust even deeper.

Fuck.

"That's a good boy," he whispered. "This throat was made to be bred by me, wasn't it?"

I tried to nod, tears streaming. The hot water from the shower pelted my back, rolling down my body. He grunted as he drew back, saliva dripping down my chin as I gulped in air.

"Good," he praised.

He grabbed my jaw and forced it open again, looping his thumb in my cheek and tugging.

"Take another deep breath for me."

I did as he asked. He waited until I breathed out before he grabbed the head of his cock and pressed it against my mouth again, shoving forward. I cried out around him as he filled me, my fingers raking down his beefy thighs.

"Relax."

I tried. I fought him for a few moments longer before something changed. It was like a switch flipped in my mind, and everything became easier. I stopped struggling against him, submitting fully to what he wanted. He drove deeper, fucking my throat with his Minotaur cock.

"Gods, you feel so fucking good. You're gripping me like a vice."

He yanked his cock free and reached for the shower, turning off the water.

"Stand up," he said.

I licked my lips as I rose. He grabbed a couple of fluffy towels and dried the two of us off quickly. He slipped his hand in mine and led me to the bedroom. He had a massive California king sized bed with a black leather headboard and dark blue bedding. All the windows were curtained, keeping any prying eyes from spying on us.

He shoved me back onto the bed, and I stumbled, landing in the middle. I licked my lips, tasting the remnants of precum.

"I need you," I said.

"You have me."

I drank in his Minotaur form, enjoying how monstrous he looked right now. He was tall, his muscles sculpted, and cock throbbing. He snapped his fingers and one of the lamps turned on, casting a golden halo over us.

I reached down and stroked my cock, watching him as he went to the side table and pulled out a bottle of lube.

"Stay here," he said. "All that fucking in the Labyrinth was wonderful, but I missed a couple of things…"

I raised a brow as he tossed me the bottle of lube and then left the room. I wondered what he was going to bring back. I poured some of the liquid into my palm and turned onto my side, working some of it into myself.

I couldn't wait to feel his cock inside of me again.

There was so much tension from the last…couple of days? Weeks? I felt like we'd stepped out of time while together.

With everything that was about to happen and had been realized, I needed to feel the connection with him.

Ryan came back into the rooms with a set of leather cuffs and a blindfold. I smirked as he came to the edge of the bed. I held out my wrists for him and he cuffed them. He then slipped the silk blindfold over my eyes, the darkness a comfort.

He moved me with little to no effort. One moment I was spread out, the next I was on my knees, my ass facing him, chest pressed into the soft blankets. He reached around and grabbed a pillow, sliding it beneath me for extra support.

"Such a gentleman," I whispered.

"A gentleman who's about to fuck you so hard you forget who you are."

"Please," was all I could say.

The blindfold kept me from seeing anything, which made me listen and feel more intensely. I sank into the position he'd put me in, feeling the submission of it, reveling in that I was giving myself to him completely.

"You look so good when you're obedient, little king," he whispered.

The bed moved behind me as he climbed on, kneeling. I listened to the sound of his breaths and the lube he poured onto his cock. Anticipation built as I waited, my own cock rigid and throbbing as Ryan pressed himself against my waiting hole.

He gripped my hips, holding me still as he pushed forward. I spread around him, his cock hot as he pushed into me in one swift motion.

"Fuck," I whimpered.

It didn't matter how many times I took him, that first thrust was always so much. I groaned as pleasure curled through me, mixed with a bit of pain and adjusting to his size. He waited a moment, giving me time to relax. The moment he felt me relax, he pulled back out and then drove back in again.

I wanted him to mate me.

I leaned back into him, grunting as he fucked me. With every pump, all I could think about was sealing this bond that we clearly had.

I wanted to know him forever. I wanted the two of us to do this forever. That feeling hadn't just been because we were trapped in the labyrinth together.

It went beyond that.

"Mate me," I rasped.

Ryan froze, his breath hitching.

"I mean it," I said. "I want this. I want you. I want you to mate me."

"If I do, then it's a bond that lasts forever. It will make us even closer than either of us know..."

"I want this," I huffed. "If you do..."

He slapped my ass hard and pulled out of me, pushing me over onto my back. He leaned down and yanked up the blindfold, staring down at me as if to make sure I meant what I said.

I held his fiery eyes. "I mean it. I want you. I want this."

"Grim..." he trailed off, his gaze softening. There was some pain there, too, but I couldn't understand why.

"You don't want me," I whispered, feeling a sense of horror. "I'm sorry I asked. I'm not trying to pressure you. I thought—"

"Grim, shut the fuck up. Right now."

I snapped my mouth shut.

He snorted and smoke shot from his nostrils. He closed his eyes and then shook his head, opening them to look at me again. "Of course I want this. Of course I want to mate you. I want you forever. I want to be yours and for you to be mine. Everything I have, I want to give to you. I want to please you, fuck you, kiss you, seduce you, charm you, love you. You don't know how long I've waited to feel like this about someone. I never believed I would. I never thought there was anyone out there for me. I never thought anyone would love me because I don't deserve to be loved."

"Everyone deserves love," I said softly. "Even you. Even me."

It took everything in me to hold back tears. His hands loosened on me and he leaned down, kissing me passionately.

"I'm going to mate you," he whispered. "I'm going to mate you and I'm going to love you and cherish you and show you what it means to live without being scared. Even if I'm fucking scared too."

I leaned up and kissed him again, wrapping my arms around his neck. I needed to hold him, to feel him around me.

He pushed my legs apart and shoved his cock inside of me again. The two of us groaned together as he kissed down my neck. I'd never realized how sharp his teeth were until he parted his jaws and sank them into my shoulder.

I cried out. Euphoric pleasure slammed into me so hard that I immediately came, my cum splashing onto Ryan as he pumped into me. He groaned as he took my blood, holding his wrist to my lips and offering it to me.

Was I supposed to bite him too?

I grunted as my orgasm washed over me, the waves of pleasure stunning me. I bit into his wrist hard enough that the skin tore, the taste of his blood hitting my tongue.

What is this?

There were no words to describe it. The pleasure, the connection, the way his soul bared itself to mine in all of its scars, ugliness, and beauty—and how it mirrored my own, answering the call I'd been screaming for so long. Someone else that was mine, that loved me for my flaws, and could take me as I was. Someone that wanted a better life and to change for the good.

My mate had centuries of begging and yearning and so much pain that I started to cry again, feeling what he hid so damn well.

Ryan pulled back, the bite wound starting to heal. We stared at each other and didn't need words.

I could feel him.

He thrust forward, and we both gasped together. Everything ran deeper now. His desires and rapturous pleasure intertwined with my own, driving him harder. He groaned and planted his hands on either side of me, driving in and out of me slowly.

"Fuck," he rasped. "I can feel everything."

I could too.

I held onto him as he kept moving, a soft moan leaving us as he came closer to the edge. Within a few moments, he let out a low growl and started to come, the heat rushing inside me.

He pressed his forehead to mine. I couldn't help but smile, thinking that maybe some things happened for a reason.

And that I was thankful he was mine.

Chapter 16

Moonie's

Ryan

For the first time in what felt like ages, I shifted back into my human form. It was easier to move around the apartment that way. I could hear Grim rummaging in the kitchen, although he wouldn't find much. We'd need to order something.

I sat down in my office and pulled open my email, curious to see what I'd missed. According to the time and date, Grim and I were gone for two and a half weeks.

It could have been worse.

I blew out a soft whistle. My email was blown up, and there was a very heated exchange on the monstrous side. I clicked through and then sat back.

There was a meeting tomorrow morning at 8 A.M.

I stared at the date and leaned back in my chair.

Grim came to the doorway and leaned against it. He wore a black silk robe and looked like a king. I patted my thigh, and he smiled as he came to me.

"I'm not used to this form of yours," he teased.

I pulled him onto my knees and gestured at the screen. He leaned forward and nodded.

"So, we show up. Announce that we're alive. Expose Theseus."

"Yes," I said. "That's my thought as well."

"Or…"

"Or?" I echoed.

He twisted around and looked at me. "Or…You could go to the meeting and I could rescue Valerie. And then we could head there, where we can prove what Theseus has done."

"Is Valerie completely unable to leave?" I asked.

He winced. "I'm not sure. It depends on if she's being punished for something."

I shook my head, that fierce rage rekindling. "He has fallen far from the hero he once was."

"He's a bastard," Grim muttered.

I agreed.

"If we go together, that will be enough proof, and the rest of the mafia can enforce her release," I said. "I know that you want to make sure she is safe, but I think that if we go together, it will be powerful."

He weighed what I said and then nodded. "We will do that then. And I'll try not to kill him."

"You and me both," I muttered. I rested my chin on his shoulder, breathing in his scent. "We should rest for a couple of hours. And then I will call one of my men to arrange things."

"Can they be trusted to not say you're alive?"

I thought about Jeff and nodded. "He's loyal. Based on the emails I just read, they have been hunting for me. Theseus and the Chimera Twins lied about your existence, and it seems like Damon hasn't brought it up yet. He's probably waiting to see if it can be used as leverage."

Grim sighed and melted into me. "A couple of days ago, all I remembered was how glorious your cock was. I didn't give two shits about the mafia or the city. But now I remember everything, and I do care."

"It's a lot to process," I whispered.

"It's too much and not enough at the same time. I'd completely forgotten that my friend exists."

"You can't feel guilty, Grim. Theseus manipulated you. He has been manipulating you for almost half your life."

He made a little noise, pressing his lips together. "Well, when you put it that way…it helps a little."

"Good. Do you remember it all?"

He was silent and then shook his head slowly. "No. Not entirely. Most of my memories have come back, but…I did so much bad. I've done so many terrible things. And the last six months I've been living in this bubble of ease without even realizing it. I'm glad Hades freed me, but I'm also angry about it."

"His interaction with you was far kinder than I've heard about any other godly interactions."

"Well…I'm still coming to terms with the fact that I met my father."

"You're coming to terms with a lot."

I tightened my arms around him and lifted him, enjoying the squeak he made as I carried him out of the office and back to the bedroom. I plopped him in the center of our bed and crawled in next to him, pulling the blankets around us. He chuckled as I bundled us up.

"Sleep, little king," I whispered. "Tomorrow, we will change everything for the better. Theseus' will lose his golden crown and it'll belong to you."

He curled into me, his arms wrapping around my body and holding me close. He was tense for a couple of minutes until finally, he breathed out and relaxed completely. It wasn't long after that before he fell fast asleep.

* * *

I slept for two hours, but it was enough to give me the energy I needed to get everything ready for Grim and I to go to the meeting. By the time he woke and came into the living room, I was back in my human form, dressed in a suit that spoke power, and had Moonie's on the kitchen bar thanks to Jeff.

Grim let out a low groan as he stretched. I admired my mate as I took a sip of coffee.

"I need to shower and get ready. But I don't know what I should wear. I don't have anything."

"I have a suit for you," I said with a smirk.

He gave me a quizzical glance. "Really?"

"I'm guessing it'll fit. It's hanging up in the bathroom. And Jeff brought breakfast..."

"Whoever Jeff is, I like him," he chuckled. He crossed the living room to me and leaned down, kissing me on the lips. He let out a soft hum and kissed me again, this time deeper.

I gave him a playful push. "Get ready before my brain stops working and we miss the meeting."

"Yes, Sir," he teased.

He went to the bar and let out a pleased groan. "Moonie's?"

"You know it?" I asked, twisting in my chair.

"Only the best godsdamned cinnamon rolls in Moirai," he snorted.

He grabbed the bag off the counter and came back to me. I set my coffee down on a small side table as he sat in my lap.

"Grim," I said. I wasn't sure if saying his name was a warning or a plea.

"I'll behave," he said. "Would hate to ruin this expensive suit."

I gave him a flat look, and he snorted as he reached into the bag and pulled off a piece of the cinnamon roll. I enjoyed the way his eyes fluttered as he took a bite.

"We'll defeat them with ease because we'll both be on a fucking sugar high."

I snorted and reached up, thumbing away icing from the corner of his mouth and sucking it off.

"Tell me what our plan is," he said.

"I'll tell you while you shower," I said. "Go on, and I'll check in with Jeff and be right there."

He kissed my cheek and got up, retreating to the bathroom. I heard the shower turn on and smirked. It was no use. Stressed or not, I was going to think about him being wet and naked.

A soft knock at the door four times in a row echoed, the signal from Jeff. I got up and opened it slightly.

"Everything is ready for you, sir," he said. "I've ensured that no one knows you're back."

"Thank you," I said.

He gave a curt nod. "I'll be waiting here for you."

"And my mate. Grim. When you meet him, know that whatever he requests, he gets."

"Yes, Sir."

I shut the door and then strolled through the apartment and down the hall. I stepped into the bathroom, grateful that the shower was made of glass and I could see everything.

"We will not tell everyone about Paris and Ty," I said. "The Chimera Twins."

Grim scoffed and turned around as he lathered up shampoo. "Why?"

"Because I want leverage over them. They know that if they're exposed in that manner, the others will be furious. They will want that kept secret if possible. We can use that against them in the future."

He pressed his lips together. "So we pin it all on Theseus?"

"Yes. Everything on him. And if Paris and Ty confess to being involved, we'll roll with it."

"What'll happen then?" he asked.

"It's tough to say exactly. More than likely, he'll get into a lot of trouble. No one will want to work with him and it'll make running his territory a lot harder."

"That's it?" Grim scoffed. "A slap on the wrist?"

I pressed my lips together. It wasn't the vengeance either of us truly wanted, but it would do more damage than Grim realized.

"More than anything, I want to walk into this meeting and rip his throat out. I'd love to watch him bleed out on the floor and fucking die," I said. "We have to trust the Fates."

I could feel his frustration simmering as he flipped off the shower and stepped out to dry off.

"I worry that if we don't end him now, he'll continue to do terrible things."

"Do you want to kill him?"

Grim bundled himself in a fluffy towel and crossed to me. I reached up and slid my fingers through his beard, gripping his chin. His eyes darkened as they met mine.

"I want to," he whispered. "But I won't. Just maybe maim him a little."

"Good. We'll do this. We'll make him agree to set Valerie free. And the other demigod if possible. Then, we'll let everyone else make their own decisions, and we'll start our life…" As I said the last of that, my throat tightened.

He was my mate now. We'd made that connection, but I'd never really talked about the implications.

The corner of his mouth tugged. "You want me to move in, hmm?"

I blushed. "Maybe..."

He leaned up on his toes and kissed me. "Just maybe?"

"Get fucking dressed," I hissed.

He smirked and kissed me once more. "I'll be ready in five and then we can go kick some crusty demigod ass."

Chapter 17

Revenge

rim

I was dressed in a navy coat that whipped in the wind, black dress pants, black oxfords, a silk black shirt, and a belt that had an array of knives tucked into it. Ryan was loaded, too. As we got out of the car, he gave me one last glance.

"I love you," he said.

"I love you too," I mumbled.

He smiled, and then his expression became cold. His muscles tensed as he readied himself for our confrontation.

I felt like a badass as we shoved through the rusty doors of a metal building outside Moirai City at 8:03 A.M.—which meant the mafia meeting had started.

I stalked after Ryan, who moved with a fierceness that even made me shiver. The rage between us was strong enough that any of the other mafia guards simply stepped back at our appearance, their eyes widening.

A long dark hall led to another door, and behind it I could hear the shouting. I could feel the frustration, the fear, the high emotions pouring out.

Ryan slowed and turned, meeting my gaze.

I gave him a nod.

I was ready.

He let out a low growl and kicked open the doors, stepping into the hostile room. I stepped in behind him and silence fell over, the mouths of our enemies falling open.

The satisfaction ran deep.

"Ryan," one of them whispered. I recognized him as the dark-haired Chimera Twin, Paris. He shook his head, giving his brother a look that was drenched in rage.

"You're alive, thank the gods." A man with short, almost black hair stood from his seat and immediately clasped Ryan in a hug.

"Damon," Ryan greeted softly. He glanced across the room at a man with iridescent eyes and gray hair. "Ian."

Damon's gaze flickered to mine, curiosity clearly there. He stepped back to his seat. "Since you're here, sit. We will hold a full meeting. Everyone is here." Next to him were two other men and a woman with blonde hair. Her eyes immediately went to mine.

She was a demigod.

As was the woman seated next to Ian. She had long dark hair and tan skin, and an aura of fierce power.

Theseus hadn't seen me yet, as I was still slightly behind my mate. I stepped around Ryan, revealing myself to the rest of the room, and the expression he made brought me more joy than almost anything else ever had.

"We have a lot to discuss," Ryan snarled. "A fucking lot of betrayals and backstabbing in this room."

"Nonsense," Theseus hissed.

"Shut the fuck up, Theseus," one Chimera twin growled.

Ryan slipped his hand into mine, a display that sent a series of rumblings through the room. He led me to an empty seat and pulled it out for me.

"I'll stand," he said. "First, let me introduce everyone in the room to Grim. Grim is the son of Hades. A demigod, like several in this room. And there are others like him we didn't know about. But Theseus did."

All eyes turned to Theseus. His cheeks were turning tomato red, the veins bulging in his neck and head. "You're a liar and deceiver."

"I am?" Ryan asked. "I'd introduce Grim to you, but he already knows you. He's known you since you bought him when he was a sixteen-year-old, trained him to fight and kill and to do your dirty work. Just like you trained another demigod named Valerie for the same reason. And not to mention, you traded another to a monster that could be in this very room."

The silence was loud. I glanced around, noting three men that sat close together had tensed significantly. One of them met my gaze, and I fought the urge to suck in a panicked breath. I could feel his darkness. Death clung to him.

"This is preposterous," Theseus snarled. "Why would I ever—"

I slammed my hand on the table, and the lights flickered. "Because you hate the monsters," I said, holding his bright blue gaze. "That's what you taught us. And you sent me to assassinate Ryan in the Labyrinth, a club that you own and regularly use for underhanded dealings. But that's not what happened. He's my mate. And that broke whatever fucking mind control you've been using to keep me in line. And I ran."

His lips lifted in a snarl, and he leaned forward. "You're a nobody. No one here believes you. You're not one of us."

"I am not one of you," I agreed. "But I am one of them." I gestured to Ryan and his hand settled on my shoulder, offering me the strength I needed to speak to the man that had abused me and used me for years. As I talked, I remembered more, and those memories were darker and graver, but I couldn't let them take me down.

I couldn't let him win.

My voice strengthened as I spoke. "You taught me to hate monsters, and I do hate monsters. I fucking hate you. I hate everything that you've done to me, to Val, and to the other demigod I never even met. You are the monster in this room."

He started to rise, but Ryan was quick. He moved in a blur, shoving Theseus back into his seat. He leaned in, his eyes burning like twin flames.

"Let's talk about how you tried to assassinate a member of the Three Fates Mafia. And then how you trapped me in the real Labyrinth. Again. After the Fates chose me."

"They made a mistake!" Theseus thundered.

A man sitting next to him shook his head. "Theseus, stop."

"Be silent, Orpheus. Everyone knows how much you loathe them. The Fates made a mistake with all of you! And the demigod whore is having children with monsters?! It's horrible! Those children will be horrid beasts, just like the Minoan Bull."

If there was anger in the room before, it felt like nothing compared to now. Ian slowly stood up while growling, as did Damon and the two men next to him.

Damon let out a low snarl. "Have you been hunting new demigods? You have one chance to be honest with us."

"Confess and then he is mine," Ian said.

The calmness in his voice was concerning. For Theseus.

Personally, I enjoyed its ominousness.

Theseus glowered. His gaze swept to mine. "You can't save your friend from her fate. You and Valerie were always scheming—"

"THESEUS!" Ian roared. "Answer the godsdamned question."

Ryan stepped back, coming back to me. I stood up slowly, moving the chair aside so I could lean into him.

We'd set the pieces on the table and now it was time to see how they fell.

Theseus stood up slowly and planted his hands on the table. "I have watched this world grow and change for hundreds of years. When the Fates created this absurd mafia with monsters, they made their greatest mistake. The purpose of demigods is to eliminate every single one of you. You're beasts. You're creatures the gods loathe. You deserve nothing but misery. Yes. Yes, I've been finding new blood and training them. This one is clearly a failure."

Something about the way he said that snapped something inside of me. One moment I was standing in front of Ryan, and the next moment, I was standing behind Theseus with my hand through his chest, gripping his beating heart.

Gold blood dripped on the table as he wheezed.

"One movement and I could reap your soul," I whispered. "The way you had me reap souls over and over again for years of people who didn't deserve it."

"Grim," Ryan warned. "Remember."

Remember what Hades had said. He wasn't mine to kill, and yet...I could feel the organ pulsing in my palm. It would be so easy to end this. So easy to get my revenge and send him to the pits of hell where Charon could have fun torturing him.

"Agree that you will set Valerie free immediately," I said. "You will call her while in this room and let me speak to her. And you agree that if the monster who harbors the other demigod is in this room, they'll release her."

"I can't make agreements for others," he growled.

"Do you want to live?"

Everyone stared as the lights flickered again, the darkness swelling around me. There was so much power in holding his life so close to death, and I was teetering on the edge of taking things too far. The man in front of me had done so much bad.

"I agree," Theseus spat out. "Valerie will be free. I can't speak for the other demigod."

"We'll find her, Grim," Ryan said.

"Release him," Orpheus growled at me.

I smiled softly and leaned in, keeping my voice low. "Obedience suits you, Theseus. There are creatures in hell that are eager for your arrival," I whispered. "But not today, and not by my hand."

I released him and he fell forward, clutching his chest as he panted. "You'll regret this," he rasped.

"Call her," I growled.

He reached into his pocket and drew out his phone. I couldn't help but notice the slight tremble in his hand as he hit a contact and handed the phone to me.

I took it and glared at him.

"Yes, Theseus?" Valerie's voice answered.

"Val," I breathed. "It's Grim."

"Grim? You're alive? Where the fuck—wait, how the fuck do you have—"

"He has released us," I said. It took every ounce of power now to hold back tears. I wouldn't cry in a room full of mafia monsters. "It's done. We did it."

She was quiet. Her words trembled as she spoke. "You're lying."

"I'm not, Val. I can't stand here and keep convincing you. I'm in a room full of demigods and monsters. Meet me at our old spot. It's done."

I hung up before she could get another word in and handed the phone back to Theseus.

"She'll be nothing without me," he sneered.

"One more fucking word out of your mouth, and I'm ripping your tongue out," Ryan growled. "Or maybe Grim can grab your heart and rip it out. That would be even more entertaining."

Ian rolled his shoulders back, his form already shimmering. Scales bloomed over his skin, his face becoming dragon-like. "You're going to fucking regret calling my wife a whore," he said. "This meeting is over. I will take Theseus with me unless any of you want to end up on the fucking floor."

Theseus looked up at Paris and Ty. "Help me," he whispered.

Ty stood up with a short, cocky laugh. "You've angered the Colchian Dragon. Who are any of us to stand in the way? His wife is the daughter of Ares. I'm sure she'd love to watch you bleed."

His gaze met mine. I couldn't help but smile. I fought the urge to ask him if he'd replaced his phone.

"Wait," Orpheus said, standing up. "There is an unresolved issue of Medusa's part of the mafia."

"Madeline," several people in the room corrected.

"For fuck's sake," Damon muttered, rubbing his temples. "Someone email the fucking Fates and ask them. We're done for today. We have a fucking city to run. Business to see too. This was a fucking far better outcome than what I was prepared for."

"How many times can you say fuck?" a man asked as he stood. Damon gave him a dark look, which only made him grin.

"Team Cerberus and Ashely are out. May Theseus' guts rain down on Moirai."

Theseus started to rush around the table for the doors, but Ian met him with ease, grabbing him by the throat and dragging him out of the room. The woman with dark hair shot me a wink and followed after him.

"Oh, I want to watch," the other blonde demigod chimed. "We'll talk another time, Grim."

Orpheus got up quickly and stormed out, and so did everyone else aside from myself, Ryan, and the Chimera Twins.

The doors swung shut, the silence deafening.

"What we did was wrong," Paris said.

"We had our reasons," Ty muttered.

"I have a question," Ryan said. "How were you able to access the real Labyrinth?"

"It was Theseus. He has access somehow. We never asked," Ty said.

"Yes, and we should never have aligned with Theseus. Why didn't you tell the room? They would have wanted to know that we were part of this, and yet you kept it from them," Pais asked.

"You know why," Ryan growled. "You owe me. You owe Grim. That's why."

There was a heavy silence, but they both nodded.

"Fair enough. Be well," Ty said.

Ryan and I were quiet as they left. I blew out a breath, looking down at my hand coated in gold blood.

"We need to meet Valerie," I sighed. "She'll have so many questions."

"We'll go," he said immediately. "What's your old spot?"

I stared at him for a moment and then felt everything soften. My shoulders relaxed as I finally breathed out. I crossed the room to him and he tugged me close, tipping my chin up.

"You can't relax yet," he whispered. "We'll go see your friend and then we're going to have a proper date."

I raised a brow. "A proper date?"

"Yes." He smirked. "I am a romantic, you know?"

"You're also a sexy brute."

"That too. As are you. You had Theseus shaking in his boots. It turned me on."

I barked out a laugh. "Of course it did."

He planted a kiss on my lips and then gestured to the doors. "Come on. Let's go find your friend. Where are we going, anyway?"

"Moonie's, ironically," I snorted. "It's the only place we ever went where no one bothered us."

Chapter 18

Golden Seal

Grim

The drive to Moonie's was quick. I realized I could get used to someone else driving for me. Jeff pulled us into a tight parking spot with the ease of someone who knew Moirai, and I opened the door, stepping out into a morning that felt good for once.

"I'm going in alone," I said. "If that's okay."

Ryan nodded. "I'll be here."

I winked at him and shut the door. When I turned, I glimpsed myself in the windows of the tiny shop. I looked different. The suit fit me well, and there was a lightness to the way I walked—as if misery had finally released me from its painful grip.

There was a line out the door, but it was the alley behind the place that Val would meet me.

I slipped between the two buildings and made my way

down the alley. A slender hand grabbed me, but the strength behind it was far from fragile.

Valerie slammed me against the brick wall, holding a knife to my throat.

I snorted. "Really, Val?"

"What do you mean, really? You've been gone for six fucking months," she snarled.

She was frazzled. I'd known her long enough to know how she reacted when she was scared, and that call earlier had scared the shit out of her. Her amber hair was braided into plaits and pulled back, and she wore the clothes we did when we were out to kill. Nondescript, easy to move in. Her dark brown eyes flickered with doubt as she studied me.

"It's me," I whispered. "And I can't die. Hades is my father."

"You've never known who..."

"I met him. A lot has happened. Are you going to stab me? Or are you going to celebrate the fact that I beat Theseus?"

Her grip tightened on my collar, the knife pressing in more. She studied me, as if weighing whether I was being truthful. Finally, she released me, taking a step back.

"You always said we would do it," I insisted. "That we'd become stronger than him. And I did. Six months ago, do you remember him sending me out?"

"Of course I do. That was the last time I saw you. Heard from you. I thought he killed you, Grim. I tore up the prison cells, the chambers, every property he owns looking for you. When I couldn't find you, I started hunting for you...I guess you didn't get my message."

"Your message?" I asked.

"There was this guy Theseus sent me to kill on the east docks. He wanted me to interrogate him. He suspected you were using that place as a hideout."

The BEWARE painted on the wall...

Things made more sense now. Of course, they hadn't then. I hadn't even remembered who I was.

"The mechanical dogs?" I asked. "Were those yours?"

She nodded, pressing her lips into a thin line. "When you left, he started using me more. He made me build him an entire army of them. They're deadly beings. Fast. Can't really die. They move in a pack."

I swallowed hard, wondering what Thesues would do with them now. While we weren't sure exactly who her godly parent was, I suspected it was Hephaestus. Valerie had an ability with mechanical things that was unnatural, such as breathing life into them.

"I don't know why you didn't come to me," she hissed. "Why didn't you?"

"I'm sorry," I whispered. "I didn't remember...His plan worked. When we leave him, we forget who we are."

"Fuck," she sighed. "I always hoped he was lying about that."

I shook my head. "I forgot everything. I forgot I was a demigod, that I had any sort of power. The last six months, I was hiding and running but didn't even realize why. Hades lifted whatever enchantment he used on me so that I could remember. The night I went to the Labyrinth, I was supposed to kill Ryan Maddock, who actually turned out to be the Minoan Bull...and my fated mate."

"Your what?"

"Fated mate. Ryan. We're basically married." I fought the urge to laugh, because in a way, it sounded absurd. But it had become my new normal.

She gave me a very flat expression. "You married a Minotaur?"

I grinned. "I did. He's pretty fucking hot, too."

"We're supposed to kill monsters," she sighed. "Not end up fated to them."

"That's what Theseus wanted us to believe, but...I met two other demigods that have monstrous mates and they seem happy. Not all monsters are bad. And so, Theseus turned against him, had us thrown into the Labyrinth, and we got out, and now here I am after a meeting with the entire Three Fates Mafia. Theseus is done with us."

"He'll never be done with us," she whispered. Her expression darkened, and she looked away.

"He is. He set us free. We're done with him."

"He might be done with you," she said. "But he will never be done with me. Why didn't you kill him?"

I let out a slow breath, leaning back against the wall. "He wasn't mine to kill."

"That's bullshit. You had the chance and you let that monster walk free?"

"Val, there's more to everything than just that. Why don't you come stay with me? Ryan and I have plenty of space. You'd be safe. He can't hurt you."

She crossed her arms, but she was at least considering it.

"Please," I whispered. "I'm sorry I left you. I couldn't remember anything until literally like a day ago. Everything has changed in the last few days. I just want you to feel safe."

She offered me a genuine smile, that cold exterior finally melting some. "You sound different, you know. Like..."

"Happy?"

"Yeah, actually," she snorted. "It's weird."

"Yeah, I don't think I've ever been happy until now."

"How does it feel?" She grinned at me.

I chuckled. "Fucking good. Really fucking good."

"Good," she said.

"So..."

I frowned as her eyes visibly darkened, and she stumbled back, her knife clattering to the ground. I picked it up and reached for her, concerned.

"Val, what's wrong?"

She took a step back with a gasp, her eyes widening at me. "Leave me alone!" she shouted.

"Val, what's going on?" I asked, reaching for her again.

She took another few steps back, throwing up her hands in defense. "I don't know you."

Fuck.

FUCK. This couldn't be happening. Panic reared its ugly head as I took a step closer to her.

"Val, listen to me. You know me. Theseus must have...fuck. He must have done something to activate the memory thing that happened to me—"

"You're fucking crazy," she growled. "Get away from me!"

"Val!"

"Stay away!"

She spun and took off down the alley. I chased after her, cursing as I came out onto the sidewalk, looking both ways.

She'd always been faster than me. And, memories or not, she'd always been able to hide better too.

Damn it.

I should have realized it could happen to her. That's what Theseus had meant when he said I'd regret having him set her free.

"Gods damn it," I snarled.

Ryan got out of the car quickly and slammed the door shut, coming to me. "Grim? What's wrong? Was that woman Val?"

"Did you see what way she went?" I asked.

"She went into the crowd and disappeared. What the fuck happened? Also, maybe put away the knife?"

We were getting worried glances. I cursed under my breath and slipped it into my jacket, looking around.

"Fuck," I sighed. "Something happened. It was like...we were talking and then she suddenly didn't remember who I was. Who she was. Theseus' curse must have activated somehow."

"I have a good description of her. I could have my men be on the lookout."

He could try. He could have the whole Three Fates Mafia on the lookout for her. It wouldn't help.

The same way it hadn't helped when I didn't want to be found, either.

Theseus had trained us well.

I ran my fingers through my dark hair, worry and stress making my muscles tense. I'd had her right there, but she'd slipped through my fingers.

"Hey," Ryan said softly, reaching up to pull me close. I leaned into him, his comfort yet again keeping me from completely unraveling. "She'll be okay. We'll keep a look out for her. But if she's anything like you, she'll be okay. And she can't hide for too long. Not in this city."

"She might leave," I whispered.

"She won't," he sighed. "Not unless the Fates let her. Moirai is a trap for beings like us."

That was the truth. It had worked out for me, at least, and all I could do was hope it would work out for Val.

"Let's go home," he whispered.

I nodded and he led me back to the car. He opened the door for me and I slipped inside, waiting for Ryan to get in on the other. The moment he did, Jeff cleared his throat in the front seat and held up a black envelope with a golden wax seal.

"Sir, this was at the house and I was asked to give it to you now," he said.

"Who asked you?" Ryan growled.

"A woman. I can't remember her."

We glanced at each other, and I took the black envelope, leaning into Ryan. The golden seal had an eye on it.

"The Fates," he whispered.

Dear **GRIM**,

You have followed your path, and now it splits in two. You must make a decision. We formally offer you a place within the Three Fates Mafia. Not just as a mate to Ryan, the Minoan Bull, but as a leader with a distinct faction and responsibilities. With that, you will receive wealth, power, protection, and anything else you might need.

You would be bound to us until your duty is fulfilled, however long that may be.

Or.

You can leave the city and this world behind.

The choice is yours.

Clotho, LacHESis, and Atropos
Three Fates Mafia

Chapter 19

Decisions

Ryan

My stomach fluttered as Grim leaned back in the seat, his hand holding mine tight enough that it was clear I couldn't escape.

Every scenario that ran through my head ended with him leaving.

The Fates had given him a choice in their letter. It had been clear and concise. He could join the Three Fates Mafia and become one of us, or he could leave and never have to live this life. He had a choice, one that could take him away from me, mate or not.

I read it over his shoulder another three times, dread icing my veins.

I wouldn't blame him if he left. This morning had just been a taste of how brutal our world could be. Theseus had used him, abused him, and had done the same to his friend. And hardly anyone batted an eye at it, because one must be brutal to survive in this world.

"Grim," I whispered, my stomach twisting.

"Let's go home," he said. "Just...let me think."

"Okay." I met Jeff's gaze in the rearview. He gave a curt nod and our car lurched into traffic, heading straight for the house outside the city.

It took about an hour before the tires hit the gravel driveway. It felt like the longest hour of my entire life. And in those sixty minutes, Grim had only stared out the window, thinking things through as he watched the city pass us by.

I could feel his emotions as they rose and fell. His grief, his sadness, his anxiety.

He was my mate. I'd fallen so fucking hard for him I would do anything to keep him—except this. I wouldn't force him to join this world, even if I desperately wanted him to stay.

Even if he was mine.

I would let him go if that was what he asked of me. It would be the hardest fucking thing I'd ever have to do, but for him, I would do anything.

We got out of the car silently and made our way to the massive house. My guards were back and stationed around the property, which was nice, but I could barely give them a nod of acknowledgment as Grim and I made our way up the stairs and through the front doors.

I followed him through the entry and then up to the second floor. He took a left, going to the balcony that overlooked everything. Sunlight turned his dark eyes amber brown, lighting them up like honey. His shoulders relaxed as he looked up at me, offering me a smile.

He held up the golden letter from the Fates. "I know what I want to do—"

"Listen. I need to say this first," I rasped, grabbing his shoulders.

I had to get this out before he told me was leaving. I needed him to hear what I had to say.

"I need you to know. I know that you're my mate. I know you were made to be mine, and that I was made to be yours. I am a monster that has done terrible things through the centuries, but when I'm with you, I feel like I'm seen in a different way. You see me for who I wish I was. And—"

"I see you as who you are, Ryan. Not who you wish to be. I'm staying."

Everything else I'd planned to say vanished. My breath left me and I stared at him, speechless.

He grinned now and leaned up on his tiptoes, cupping my face. "You're such an idiot. Did you think I was going to leave? After everything we've been through?"

"It's dangerous," I whispered hoarsely. "This world is hard. Today sucked, and it could have been much worse. And your friend..."

"She'll be okay," he said. "And everything else? I have the great Minoan Bull at my side. I'm the son of Hades who can't be killed. My fate is to be with you, and if that means also running part of this world, then I'll do it. With you."

"With me," I echoed.

"Yes, you bull-headed dumbass. Did you really think you could get rid of me so easily?"

I closed my eyes, holding back tears. His grip on me tightened, and he stepped closer, his body pressing against mine.

"I love you," he said. "We've just met, but I would do anything to be with you. I want to spend the rest of my life knowing you. Learning about you. Building a future with you."

"How can you love me?"

He thumbed away a tear and chuckled. "How can I not?

And I can say the same. How can you love me? I am flawed and broken and I've done terrible things."

"How can I not?" I murmured.

He leaned up and pressed his lips to mine, cupping my face. "I want you. The monster, not the man."

I was already shifting by the end of his sentence, my muscles expanding as my body changed and turned my clothes to shreds. My horns gleamed above my head, smoke puffing from my nostrils.

He pulled the rest of my clothes off as he pushed me back down the hall towards our bedroom, his eyes lit up with lust.

"Oh?" I asked. "Is that all you want, little king?"

"Your cock in my mouth? Yes."

I let out a low growl and grabbed him, snatching him up and tossing him over my shoulder. He chuckled as I carried him to our bedroom and kicked the door shut behind me.

"What about the guards?" he asked.

"They're going to have to get used to this," I grumbled. "And maybe I'll invest in soundproofing the walls..."

"Such a generous mafia boss," he teased.

I sat him down on the edge of the bed and grabbed the collar of his shirt, ripping. The buttons popped with ease, his shirt splitting open and revealing his chest. He leaned back as I slid my hand down his stomach and grabbed the belt buckle, undoing it quickly.

"Fuck," he groaned. "I'm already fucking hard and it's just because you ripped my shirt off."

"I like monster-handling you," I grunted.

He whimpered as I pulled him to standing and quickly undressed him, moving him how I pleased. I shoved him back on the bed and followed him, pinning him beneath my body.

He ran his hands up and down my torso and then reached

for my cock. The moment he touched me, I let out a low groan, pleasure rolling through me.

"Fuck," I grunted. "I'm going to breed you until our date tonight and then we're going to go out with you full of my cum."

I slid my hand around his throat and held him in place as he stroked my cock, enjoying the hitch in his breath as I encircled his cock with my palm.

He thrust his hips up, his eyes fluttering as I tightened my grip around his neck. I could feel his pulse, his heart beat hammering against my palm.

"My mate," I rasped. "My little king. I'm going to worship you forever. I swear to the gods and the Fates and everything in this world."

His eyes watered up as I dragged him into a kiss. He reached up and grabbed hold of my horns, his lips parting as our tongues ravaged each other.

I wanted him more than anything else. I groaned as he touched me, reveling in the feeling of us being close. I could feel his pleasure through the bond, pulsing with my own.

Desire drove us. I gave him a shove, enjoying the way he leaned back onto the bed. I got up and went to the side table, quickly grabbing a bottle of lube. He licked his lips as I poured a generous amount into my palms, rubbing it up and down my throbbing cock.

The piercing at the head gleamed as I climbed onto the bed again. I grabbed onto him and moved him with ease, putting him in the position I wanted him in. I braced my hand on the headboard, enjoying the way that he pulled his legs back and readied himself for me.

"I need you," he growled. "Hard and fast."

I pressed the head of my cock against him and gave a deep thrust. His breath hitched as he took me, his lips parting on a moan. I leaned down and kissed him again, drinking him in as my cock filled him. I could feel him stretching around me, his body squeezing me like a vise.

I pulled out and then drove in again, using all of my strength as I fucked him. Bred him. Claimed him.

He was mine.

"You feel so good," he huffed, his lips parting on another groan. His cheeks flushed as he took me. "Harder."

With a grunt, I drove in hard enough that the bed creaked beneath us. Grim let out a laugh as the sound of wood snapping echoed through the room, but that wasn't going to stop me.

I fucked him deeper and faster, losing myself in him.

In taking what was mine.

In knowing that I was his, too.

Heat poured off my body in waves, surrounding the two of us in a blanket of lust as I took him. He cried out as the bed shifted, part of the frame cracking from my powerful thrusts.

"Fuck!" he groaned.

I held him in place, reaching between us to grip his cock again. I stroked as I rammed into him, feeling how near he was to coming.

The bed cracked again, and I laughed as the whole damn thing practically fell apart. Hot cum burst from his cock as he came, splashing over my body. I swiped some up with my thumb and sucked it off, the taste of him throwing me over the edge.

I roared as I came, filling my demigod mate with my cum. The heat filled him quickly, the two of us holding on to each other through the unraveling of our orgasms.

I pushed a little deeper inside of him, holding him still. I grunted as the pleasure washed over me, echoing through our connection.

Grim leaned up and kissed me, melting beneath me as I

slowly pulled out. Cum dripped out of him, making a mess on the bed. I let out a dark chuckle.

"We broke the bed," he panted. "That was amazing."

"It was," I huffed. "Looks like we have some shopping to do."

"A bed my monster can breed me on at full force without breaking in half," he snickered.

"Yes," I grinned, rolling over to the side.

His hand slipped into mine as we both stared at the ceiling, letting everything sink in.

We'd escaped the Labyrinth.

And we'd exposed Theseus.

Sort of saved his friend.

And now...

"I love you," he whispered softly, squeezing my hand gently. "I am really glad I gave you a blowjob that night at the club."

I chuckled. "Best blowjob ever."

He snickered and turned over, curling into me.

"I love you too," I said, kissing his forehead. "You're more than I could ever deserve."

"Oh, I don't know about that," he teased. "Are you going to teach me how to be a mafia boss now?"

"I will try my best. Not sure I'm the best at it."

"Between the two of us, we'll figure it out. Can't be that hard if Theseus has been doing it."

"True." I grinned now, kissing his head again. "We'll be the best we can be at it. Everyone in Moirai will come to fear you, the son of Hades."

Grim made a face. "That does sound rather frightening."

"Grim, master of death."

"Fucker of monsters."

The two of us burst out laughing. And for the first time in

my life, I finally felt like I was in the right place, with the right person, and with a future that was everything I wanted.

Mated to my demigod, a man that could see my flaws and love me anyway.

A king and his monster.

Romancing the Minotaur

Two Months Later

Grim

My Minotaur mate shivered as I tightened the chains that bound him to the St Andrew's Cross. I used a stool to reach them, one that made us the same height. The blindfold around his head was tight, keeping him from seeing what I was doing to him.

Two months of being together, and our scenes only became more intimate and intense. I grinned like the evil bastard I was as I picked up two small nipple pumps. I fit one over his left peck and then over the right one, grabbing the inflated balls at the end and squeezing.

He groaned, and his head tipped back. "Fuck," he rasped.

I watched as his nipples grew larger and larger, and left them in the spot I wanted them in. His cock pulsed, precum dripping from the tip.

"Does that feel good, little bull?" I asked.

"Yes," he whimpered.

The absolute trust we'd built together meant he let me see and love this part of him. The same monster that could rail me into next week could also be vulnerable with me, and that was beyond hot to me.

He strained against the chains as I reached out and grabbed the pumps, squeezing them both again. He groaned as I suckled him, his cock begging to be touched.

I smirked as I turned and picked up an emerald green flogger with a black marble handle. It was large and heavy, and the only way I'd been able to describe it was like being hit by a baseball bat...but in a fun way.

I swung it over my shoulder and stepped onto the stool, reaching up to loosen the chains just enough to turn him around. They crossed over each other, keeping his arms above his horned head, and the pumps pressing into the cross along with his cock as his back and ass faced me.

"What are you doing to me?" he rasped.

"Wouldn't you like to know?" I teased.

"Fuck you," he mumbled.

I grinned as I stepped down and took a few steps back, grabbing the handle of the flogger. The leather falls were dark green and heavy. I breathed in the leather scent and let out a soft hum of satisfaction before readying myself.

I drew it back and swung, hitting the left side of his back. He grunted as it impacted him, the weight of it pressing him forward. I swung again, aiming for the right side, moving back and forth between him.

"Fuck," he groaned.

The sound of the falls hitting him was hypnotic. I breathed steadily as I kept flogging him, each one more intense than the last. He shivered, panting as I kept going until finally, I tossed the flogger to the floor and stepped up behind him, pressing my cock to him. I reached around to grip his cock.

He cursed under his breath at my touch, his hips jerking.

"Good boy," I said. "Stay still."

He growled as he went still, fighting his primal instincts to thrust into my hand. I kept stroking him faster and faster until I released him, turning him around to face me again. I pulled one pump off and replaced it with my mouth, his cry echoing through the room a reward for us both.

I sucked him, swirling his swollen nipple with my tongue. His growls were involuntary, his muscles straining the urge to move. I reached up and squeezed the other pump a few times before removing it, enjoying the look he had right now.

"You're so submissive," I whispered. "The fierce Minoan Bull obeying my every whim."

I sucked the other nipple, enjoying the way those fierce growls turned to whimpers.

"Beg me to suck your cock," I demanded. "Beg for it."

He blew out a long breath, his head tipping back as I circled his nipples, teasing and pinching. "Please suck my cock. I'm begging you to please give me that honor."

My own cock throbbed as I smirked, still teasing him.

"Fuck," he shuddered, his hip thrusting out. "Please. Please, I'm begging you. I'll die if you don't suck my cock."

"Oh?" I chuckled. "So dramatic."

"Please."

I sank down to my knees in front of him, gripping the base of his shaft. He groaned, the chains jingling as I licked the head, teasing the piercing through it. The moment I tasted his precum, I felt that familiar euphoric high rushing over me, the one that always came with tasting him.

I could drink his cum all day long.

I took his cock into my mouth, sucking hard. He moaned as I took him deeper down my throat, bobbing my head back and forth. I cupped his balls as I sucked him, enjoying the pulse I could feel from him as I pleasured him. I moved back and forth, spit dripping down my chin.

A moan left me as I drew back, taking in a deep breath.

"Thank you."

Fuck. He was so fucking hot like this. I looked up at him, admiring how godly he was, how sexy.

I rose and grabbed his cock, using the stool to give me more height as I pressed his against mine. I used both of my hands to stroke them together, rubbing them simultaneously, his shaft burning hot.

"Gods," I huffed.

More precum jetted from his cock. I used it to lube ours together. His breathing came harder the faster I milked us, satisfaction washing over me in constant waves.

I leaned up and clasped onto his nipple with my mouth, sucking as I stroked. He cried out, his hips moving now, unable to stop himself.

I bit down hard, enjoying his pain.

He only pumped harder.

"Good boy," I rasped. "Keep going. Fucking hell, I love seeing you like this."

I urged him on, looking down at our cocks as we both came closer and closer.

"I can't hold back," he huffed. "Please let me come. Please."

His begging had me right there, too. "Come for me," I whispered.

He grunted, his head falling back as he gave a final thrust, hot seed gushing out in creamy ropes as I came too. I planted my hand against him, panting as our cum dripped to the floor, our bodies shuddering together.

We took a few moments to simply be, the aftermath of coming and playing better than anything else.

"Such a mess," I finally teased.

He laughed and leaned back against the cross. I reached up and pulled his blindfold free. He blinked a few times and shook his head, looking down at me.

I undid the chains quickly and was shocked as he lunged for me, lifting me with ease.

"Hey," I said, but I was already wrapping my arms around his neck and legs around his waist.

He carried me out of our fun room and through the house to the bedroom. We'd replaced the bed a second time, finally finding one that could withstand the force a demigod and monster could create. We'd also expanded the bathroom to add what was essentially a hot tub, large enough for both of us to enjoy.

For the most part, Ryan was always in his monster form now. It brought me joy. There was even a day recently where he'd gone out into the world that way, and while he'd garnered some attention, it hadn't been the terror he'd expected.

"I want a hot bubble bath," he said. "And I want you sitting in my lap while we relax."

"Now, look who's so demanding," I said. "And after you were just begging me so much."

He gave me a knowing smirk. "Well, it's our day off. We gotta enjoy every moment, which means we get to play our switchy games."

I grinned as he carried me to the bath like a princess. He let me down and turned on the water, tugging me close as we waited for it to fill.

In a world of monsters, mafia, demigods, and gods—I'd found the monster that was made for me.

On Mondays, we chose violence. Tuesdays, we worked our asses off running our businesses. On Wednesdays, we wore suits. Thursdays and Fridays, more business and Moonie's cinnamon rolls...

And the weekend?

Well, the weekend was for fucking from dusk to dawn, and romancing my mafia Minotaur mate.

Clio's Creatures

Hello Creatures!

My name is Clio Evans and I am so excited to introduce myself to you! I'm a lover of all things that go bump in the night, fancy peens, coffee, and chocolate.

 IF you had the chance to be matched with a monster or alien—what kind would you choose?!

 Let me know by joining me on FB and Instagram. I'm a sucker for werewolves (and swoony tentacle aliens) to this day.

Also by Clio Evans

Creature Cafe Series
Little Slice of Hell

Little Sip of Sin

Little Lick of Lust

Little Shock of Hate

Little Piece of Sass

Little Song of Pain

Little Taste of Need

Little Risk of Fall

Little Wings of Fate

Little Souls of Fire

Little Kiss of Snow: A Creature Cafe Christmas Anthology

Little Drop of Blood

Little Heart of Stone

Warts & Claws Inc. Series
Not So Kind Regards

Not So Best Wishes

Not So Thanks in Advance

Not So Yours Truly

Not So Much Appreciated

Freaks of Nature Duet

Doves & Demons

Demons & Doves

Three Fates Mafia Series

Thieves & Monsters

Killers & Monsters

Queens & Monsters

Kings & Monsters

Galactic Gems Series

Cosmic Kiss

Cosmic Crush

Cosmic Heat

Small Town Romance by Clio

Broken Beginnings (Citrus Cove 1)

www.ingramcontent.com/pod-product-compliance
Ingram Content Group UK Ltd.
Pitfield, Milton Keynes, MK11 3LW, UK
UKHW031841150125
4111UKWH00008B/272